I fell to the ground, twisting and thrashing, trying to squirm away, trying to fight it off. But my whole body was heavy with panic. And I couldn't breathe . . . couldn't breathe. . . .

Beside me, I saw Jamie—eyes wide, mouth locked in a wide O of horror—being strangled . . . strangled by the skeleton, a hideous grin on the dirt-caked skull.

The strong, bony hands tightened around my throat and squeezed.

Twisting to pull free, I felt something drop onto my back. And then something hit my shoulders. I saw dirt falling into the hole. Falling on my head, my back. . . .

I couldn't breathe . . . couldn't breathe at all.

The two skulls grinned. The hard, bony hands tightened and squeezed.

And the dirt rained down.

My last thought: Jamie and I . . . no one will find us.

No one will ever know where we are.

We are being strangled—*and buried alive!*

DON'T MISS A SINGLE NIGHT

#1: Moonlight Secrets

#2: Midnight Games

#3: Darkest Dawn

AND THESE OTHER CHILLING TALES FROM FEAR STREET:

All-Night Party

The Confession

Killer's Kiss

The Perfect Date

The Rich Girl

The Stepsister

FEAR STREET® NIGHTS

Moonlight Secrets

R.L. STINE

Simon Pulse
New York London Toronto Sydney

A Parachute Press Book

SIMON PULSE

An imprint of Simon & Schuster Children's Publishing Division

1230 Avenue of the Americas, New York, NY 10020

Copyright © 2005 by Parachute Publishing, L.L.C.

All rights reserved, including the right of reproduction in whole or in part in any form.

SIMON PULSE and colophon are registered trademarks of Simon & Schuster, Inc.

FEAR STREET is a registered trademark of Parachute Press, Inc.

Designed by Sammy Yuen

The text of this book was set in Bembo.

Manufactured in the United States of America

First Simon Pulse edition June 2005

10

Library of Congress Control Number 2004111512

ISBN-13: 978-0-689-87864-0

ISBN-10: 0-689-87864-8

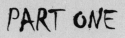

PART ONE

1

The horror started because of a kiss.

And because my girlfriend and I were somewhere we weren't supposed to be.

Jamie and I were the first Night People, although we didn't call ourselves that until much later. Soon, other kids found out about what we were doing and decided to try it too.

But in those early days, we had the whole night to ourselves—like it was *our world*! Still and quiet, and the streets all empty and the houses dark, we could go anywhere we wanted and do anything we felt like.

How cool is that?

Jamie and I started the whole thing. With mountains of homework and senior year crunch, we never had time to see each other.

So one October night we waited for our

parents to go to sleep. A little after midnight, we sneaked out of our houses and met at the construction site on Fear Street.

The old Fear Mansion was about to be torn down. All the old mansions for blocks had been knocked down to make way for the shopping center.

Fear Street Acres.

They talked about it on TV a lot. How in the past everyone in Shadyside had been scared to come to this neighborhood. How the Fear family had left some kind of evil curse on Fear Street.

But now, with Fear Street Acres, it was all supposed to change. Now the neighborhood would be jammed with shoppers and restaurants and people having fun.

The Fear Mansion was already a burned-out wreck. The brick walls were sooty and black as if a huge shadow clung to the house.

Inside, the floorboards cracked and creaked under our feet. Rats and field mice scrabbled over the floors. Insects built huge nests in the rotting walls. And the wind whistled through the broken windows.

Over a hundred years ago, there had been

a terrible fire in the house. The burned-out shell of the building had stood at the end of Fear Street ever since. A lot of people were afraid to go inside it—afraid of the curse, and of the Fear family's evil magic.

But to us, it was just a cool place to meet and hang out. Our own world. Who would look for us there?

That first night, I remember the full moon. Actually, I remember *everything* about that night. The first night of the Night People.

Jamie and I slipped into one of the abandoned houses. We found a ratty old couch to sit on, and Jamie climbed on my lap. We hardly said a word. We held each other as if we never wanted to let go. Hidden in the deep darkness, we felt safe and protected and alone.

Jamie's lipstick tasted orangy. She had her eyes shut tight as we kissed. I still remember how we started breathing so hard, and stopped, and let go of each other for a while.

We started sneaking out nearly every night.

Most nights we crept into the old Fear Mansion, and we stayed there together later and later. Around four or five in the morning, we'd sneak back to our homes and try to catch a few hours' sleep.

Some nights we explored the old house. We looked for ghosts. We looked for things that the Fears might have left. But the rooms were empty and charred and sad.

Spiders had filled the main kitchen with curtains of webs. The walls of the library were burned and peeling. Rotting bookshelves had collapsed. Our shoes slid through thick carpets of dust.

One wing of the mansion had withstood the fire. One crystal chandelier still hung in what was once the gigantic ballroom. One night Jamie and I pretended to waltz, laughing and twirling down the still-shiny floor of the enormous room.

"Wow. Lewis, just think of the parties the Fear family had here," Jamie said. "We're dancing with ghosts."

Yes, as I said, Jamie really believes in ghosts and the spirit world. Ever since her cousin Cindy died last year, Jamie has been totally obsessed.

Cindy had some kind of horrible blood disease, and she knew she wasn't going to make it. A week before she died, Jamie and I visited her in the hospital.

"I'll send you a sign," Cindy said. She had tubes in both arms and an oxygen tube in her nose. She could only whisper.

"I'll send you a sign," she said. "I'll send you a signal from the other side. I promise."

Ever since, Jamie read every book she can find about ghosts and the supernatural. She and her two friends, Christa and Elena, are all really into the ghost world. It's almost like a club. They're waiting for the signal from Cindy. Well, not just waiting. They talk about the signal and look for it everywhere.

I know Jamie liked meeting me in the Fear Mansion because she thought there were ghosts in there. She was *dying* to see a ghost, or hear one, or see some sign that they existed.

That's not why I sneaked out of my house every night. I just wanted to be with Jamie. To have our own secret world.

But, of course, our friends found out about what we were doing. And before long, Jamie and I weren't the only Night People.

Christa and Elena started sneaking out of

their houses too. And two friends of mine, Justin Schmidt and Raymond Kresge, and some guys I didn't know too well.

And then a bunch of Juniors started showing up. I remember Nate Garvin was one of the first. And then his friend Bart Sharkman—the guy everyone calls Shark. And Candy Shutt. Candy was still going with Shark then. They were totally into each other. They were always going off by themselves into one of the back rooms. Some other eleventh-grade kids came out too.

Most of us would meet after midnight at the Fear Mansion. Then we'd split up and wander off in different directions.

This was before the Nights bar opened. Nights didn't open until the next fall.

We didn't care where we met. It was just so exciting to be out all night and no one knowing about it. It was more than exciting. There was a special thrill having this secret from our parents and everyone.

Sometimes four or five of us would walk into town and stare into the dark store windows. Some nights we sneaked into the gym at the high school. We cranked up a boombox till the bleachers shook. Some nights we just hung out in the parking lot.

Shark had spray cans of that stringy stuff, and some nights he'd spray some windows or doors. He liked filling mailboxes with the stringy stuff.

Once we picked up a dog house and moved it to another yard. I don't know why we thought that was such a riot. But we did. And one night we found a dead raccoon in the road and we hung it on someone's clothes line. Dumb, huh? But kinda funny.

We never did any real damage. We didn't want to get into trouble. We didn't want to risk ruining this perfect, secret world we had.

And then came the night we found the hidden room.

There was a big crowd that night. Some of Nate and Shark's friends showed up. A girl named Ada and a couple of guys I didn't really know—Aaron and Galen Somebody.

We were all in the ballroom of the Fear Mansion. Shark disappeared into a back room with Candy Shutt. Christa and Elena hung out with Jamie and me for a while, but they went home early.

I took Jamie's arm and whispered to her. "It's too crowded tonight. Let's take a walk or something."

Jamie nodded okay.

Across the room I saw my two buddies, Justin and Raymond. They were having a friendly shoving match. Just goofing around. Justin stumbled back, laughing. I think he was trashed. He and Raymond had each brought a six-pack.

Raymond gave Justin another shove. Justin's back slammed into the wall. I heard a crash. The wall was concrete or stone. But it totally crumbled.

Justin let out a cry as the wall fell in and he crashed right through it.

"Whoa!" Raymond dropped to his knees, laughing. He dropped his can of Budweiser, and the beer splashed over the floor.

"Hey—help me!" Justin shouted. His voice was muffled by the broken wall.

I ran across the room. Jamie was right behind me. And a bunch of other kids. I bent down to see if I could pull Justin out of the wall. He was on his back, giggling and kicking his legs.

"Justin, do you want help or not?" I asked.

He cut off his laugh. "Lewis, you won't believe this," he said. "Dude, you won't *believe* this!"

And that's how we discovered the hidden room. We all followed Justin through the hole in the wall. Nate Garvin had a halogen flashlight, so we could see really well.

I squeezed through the hole and helped pull Jamie in behind me. I guess the first thing I noticed was that the room had no door. Maybe there was a trap door or something, but I couldn't find one. No door. No window.

There was no way to get into the room!

"Check this out!" Nate cried, sweeping his light over the shelves on the walls. I saw shelves going up to the ceiling, stacked high with all kinds of weird stuff.

Stacks of black candles. Jars of colored powders. Incense sticks. Animal bones. Old books and piles and piles of papers and magazines and journals. Glittery jewelry. Silver trophies and medals. A black cloak and hooded coats and long dresses hung in an alcove beside the shelves.

We all started pulling things off the shelves

and pawing through drawers like it was some kind of toy store at Christmastime. Jamie tried on a fur coat that came down to her ankles. "Feel it," she kept insisting. "Lewis, feel it." I ran my hand over the dark fur. Very soft and silky.

"Whoa—dude!" Shark showed off a tiny silver pistol he'd found. Candy found a jewelry box and started pulling out long, glittery earrings.

I found some treasures too. For one thing, a stack of old sheet music. I flipped through the pile quickly, squinting in the shifting light. Some of the songs dated back to 1900. I knew they were worth big-time bucks. And I found a two-volume coin collection that had to be worth money too.

I decided I'd hide the stuff in my room for a while, then maybe sell it on eBay.

Jamie hung the fur coat back up and went to check out the jewelry box. I saw her slip a gold bracelet on her wrist. Some of the eleventh-grade girls had found another jewelry box and were excitedly clawing through it.

"It isn't even my birthday!" Shark cried. And everyone laughed. He picked up a big, silver trophy cup. "I want to thank everyone who made this possible!" he cried. "I couldn't have done it without you!"

Guys were trying on gold and silver medals. Two girls were trading bright red, hooded cloaks. Raymond pulled a rabbit skeleton from a jar and waved it in front of Ada. She let out a scream.

Jamie came running over to me wearing long, sparkly earrings. She had a stack of old journals in her arms. "They're all about witchcraft and the supernatural," she said. "This is so cool. I can't believe Christa and Elena left early."

Well, we totally looted the place. Then, one by one, we squeezed back through the splintered hole in the wall and carried our treasures home.

Stealing?

No way you could call it stealing. No one had lived in the Fear Mansion for over one hundred years. And who knows how long the stuff had been buried in this hidden room?

Yes, it had belonged to the Fears. But the Fears were history. Now it was ours.

So we all helped ourselves. I mean, it was finders keepers, big-time.

"I'll bet this was Angelica Fear's private chamber," Jamie whispered to me. I could see she was a little frightened. Jamie believed the stories about the Fear Street curse. She believed that the evil of the Fears lived on in the house.

Not me. On that warm October night as we hurried off with our treasures, I didn't believe any of it.

Of course, a short while later—when all the horror started—I believed.

Yes, I totally believed.

2

"Lewis, did you bring your camera?" Jamie asked.

I held it up. "Maybe a ghost will pose for me over by that tree."

Jamie slapped my shoulder. "Bad attitude," she said.

I grinned at her. "Yeah, I'm feeling kinda bad." I tried to kiss her, but she backed away.

It was late October, almost Halloween, and our shoes crunched over the hard ground. Dry leaves danced around us in a sharp, gusting wind. The moon was hidden behind low clouds. Once again, we were the Night People, and the world was ours.

Tonight we returned to the grounds of the Fear Mansion. It was especially cold outside, and none of the others had made it out. But Jamie and I were there for a reason.

"I think tonight is the night I will hear from Cindy," Jamie had said as I drove her home from school that afternoon. "I just have a feeling, Lewis."

She was always having feelings about this stuff. I kept my mouth shut and tried not to argue.

"Cindy died exactly two months ago today," Jamie said, tensely twisting a strand of her dark hair. "And two was her lucky number. I know it sounds crazy. But I want to be out-side the Fear Mansion tonight watching for her signal."

"Why there? Why the Fear Mansion?" I asked.

"It was just knocked down, right?" she replied. "The ghosts have been disturbed. They'll be all around, Lewis. I know they will."

Jamie and I were there the afternoon the workers came and knocked down what was left of the Fear Mansion. We watched from across the street. It was a warm day in early fall. The leaves still shimmered green on the trees.

They used one of those giant battering balls. The ball shattered the brick walls. It didn't take long for the house to just crumble in on itself.

I had my arm around Jamie's shoulders, and I felt her whole body shake when the house came crashing down. She shut her big, brown eyes tight.

"What's wrong?" I asked.

She didn't answer for a while. A sharp gust of wind fluttered her dark hair behind her back. She shivered again.

"I just had a feeling," she said. She shrugged and gave me a smile, almost like apologizing. "A cold feeling. No big deal, Lewis."

"You think there are ghosts in there?"

"Maybe," Jamie said.

I tried to kiss her, but she turned to the house.

A thick cloud of dust rose up from the ruins of the mansion. The wind swept the dust over us, and we both spun away, coughing.

I smoothed dirt off the front of my T-shirt. Then I brushed some leaves from Jamie's blue sweater.

Workers were bulldozing what was left of

the house. The thud of bricks and the clatter of shattered glass echoed off the old trees.

It gave me a chill too. I'm not sure why.

And tonight, here we were, back on Fear Street. Because Jamie had a hunch. . . .

Would this be the night she'd finally contact the ghost world?

"There *had* to be a lot of ghosts in that house, Lewis," she said. "Their resting place has been destroyed. The ghosts will be out. The spirit power will be high. Perfect for Cindy to try to contact me."

I snickered. "Because the ghosts are *homeless*? You're joking, right?"

I could see she wasn't joking. "Forget it. You can just leave," she said sharply. "Christa and Elena will come with me."

"Hey—I'm here," I said. "I'm ready. Check it out. I brought my new digital camera, didn't I?"

So there we were, just the two of us at one in the morning, huddled in the gusting wind outside the wrecked Fear Mansion.

"You're shivering," Jamie said. She pulled the zipper on my jacket up to my neck. "Are you scared, Lewis?"

I rolled my eyes. "Huh? Yeah. Like, really. It's *cold*, Jamie. Why don't we come back in the spring and look for ghosts?"

She ignored my question and pulled a tape recorder from her backpack. She had her hair tied in a ponytail, and it got caught in the backpack strap. I pulled her hair free as she fiddled with the tape controls.

"I know you don't believe me," Jamie said. "But this is the perfect place to find someone from the spirit world. You know the stories about the Fear Mansion. Simon and Angelica Fear were supposed to be the most evil people in the world."

"We studied it all in fourth grade," I said. "I thought it was a crock back then. And so did you. Why don't you put down the recorder and come warm me up?"

She smiled. "Maybe later. Do you know about the Fears' daughters? The two little girls who were found in the woods? I mean, their skin was found, but their bones were totally gone."

I shook my head. "I *hate* when that happens."

Jamie glanced around. The wind had

stopped. A hush fell over us. I watched my breath steam up in front of me.

"There must be dozens of spirits lingering on this spot," Jamie whispered. "You know. Poor souls who were tortured by the Fears. Angelica Fear was a witch. She cast spells on a lot of people. And now their ghosts are waiting around to get revenge."

I shivered again. "How long is this going to take?" I asked.

Jamie shrugged. "As long as it takes. Cindy promised she'd send a signal. The spirit energy is so high here, Lewis. I can feel it."

We sat down on a pile of bricks, and we didn't say another word. The only sound was the soft whir of Jamie's recorder.

No wind at all. The trees around the grounds stood still and silent. No cars on the street. The houses all around lay crumbled, in ruin, ready to be carted away.

Yes, I suddenly felt creeped out.

I don't believe in ghosts. And I never really got into the stories about the Fear Family. But sitting there so silent and alert, listening and staring out into the darkness, I felt a cold tingle at the back of my neck.

"Sometimes ghosts appear as bright orbs," Jamie whispered. "Little flashes of light that you can't explain any other way."

"Have you seen any?" I whispered back.

"Not yet," she whispered.

She edged closer to me. I pressed my shoulder against hers. We sat there for a long time. My nose was getting numb, and my fingers felt frozen stiff under my gloves. I watched my breath puff up in front of me and waited.

I was being a real good sport here. Jamie was going to owe me—big-time.

"I feel something," she whispered. "I'm serious, Lewis. I sense something strange, something very close."

"I don't see anything," I whispered.

"Shhhh." She shoved me in the ribs. Her whole body went stiff. She kept her eyes straight ahead of her. "Who are you?" she called out. "I know you're here. Cindy—is it you?"

Silence.

I watched for a shiny orb of light, but I didn't see one.

"Are you there?" Jamie called, her voice just above a whisper. "Cindy? It's me. Are you there?"

No reply.

We sat there some more, breathing softly, not moving.

Finally her tape recorder made a loud click. "End of tape," she said. "Let's see if we got anything."

I clenched and unclenched my fingers, trying to get some feeling back in them. I'd been gripping the camera so hard, my fingers ached. My knees cracked as I climbed to my feet.

"I'm totally frozen," I said. "I can't stay out here in the cold listening to the tape. Besides, we didn't see or hear anything."

Jamie grabbed my arm. She pressed her cold cheek against mine. "Let's go to my house, Lewis. We can listen in my bedroom."

"You're kidding, right? If your parents catch me in your bedroom . . ."

"They're heavy sleepers," Jamie said, stepping over a pile of bricks, heading to the street. "How do you think I get out every night? It's almost three-thirty in the morning. They won't wake up till their alarm goes off at seven. Trust me."

• • •

We crept up the stairs to Jamie's bedroom, leaning hard on the banister so the steps wouldn't creak. We tiptoed into her room; it was all pale yellow and white with an old *X-Files* poster framed on the wall.

Jamie shut the door carefully. I slid my arms around her waist and started to kiss her, but she pushed me away. "Not now, Lewis. We've got to check this out."

We both dropped down on the edge of her bed. She removed the cassette from her tape recorder, turned it over, and slipped it back. Then she pushed play.

I could hear the wind on the tape. Then I heard Jamie and me talking. I was complaining about how cold I was. Then there was a long silence.

"Fast forward," I said. "There's nothing there." I reached for the tape player, but she slapped my hand away.

"Just shut up and listen. I felt something, Lewis. A presence. Maybe it was Cindy. Maybe she left something for us on the tape."

So we sat in silence and listened to the wind on the tape. I couldn't help it. I started to yawn. I wanted to curl up and go to sleep.

I felt myself drifting off . . . when the voice came on.

I sat up straight. "What was that?"

Jamie let out a gasp. She jumped to her feet, alert now. She gripped the tape player tightly in her hand. And we heard the voice again.

The voice of a ghost. . . .

3

"Back it up. Back it up," I said, my voice suddenly hoarse and breathless.

Jamie stared at me. "You heard it too?"

I nodded.

"I thought maybe I imagined it. The voice . . . it seems so far away," Jamie said. "I couldn't tell if it was Cindy or not." She rewound the tape and we listened again, pressing our ears close to the little speaker.

A roar of wind. And then a woman's voice, faint, so distant, rising over the wind.

"Mine. . . . Did you take mine?"

I think that's what she said. The voice was so soft.

I swallowed hard. My throat suddenly felt dry and tight. I grabbed Jamie's arm. "Play it again."

"Sshhh." She shook her head.

The tape rolled. Silence. Then the woman's voice again.

"... *pay. If you took what is mine, you will pay.*"

Then silence.

Jamie and I stood frozen in the middle of her room, staring at the tape player. My heart was pounding. I felt kinda light-headed, as if maybe I was dreaming this.

A voice from the *other side*?

Jamie gripped the tape player tightly. I could see that her hands were shaking.

We listened to the silence. Occasional bursts of wind.

Then I heard Jamie's voice on the tape. A whisper: "I feel something. I'm serious, Lewis. I feel something strange, something very close."

She pushed stop. "I was right," she said. "There *was* someone close. That woman. I could feel her there, Lewis. I knew I was right."

I opened my mouth, but no sound came out. I didn't know what to say. I mean, I don't believe in ghosts. At least, I didn't believe in ghosts—until then.

"Play it again," I said finally.

Jamie rewound it, and we listened to the faraway voice again. And again.

"*. . . pay. If you took what is mine, you will pay.*"

I shivered. "What does that mean? What is she saying?"

Jamie shook her head. "She sounds so angry." She set the tape player down on the bed. "It's not Cindy. Do you think maybe it's someone from the Fear family?"

"I . . . I just can't believe we recorded the voice of someone who's *dead*," I said.

We stared at each other. We were both thinking hard. Thinking about ghosts. . . .

Jamie rewound the tape, and once again we listened to the wind—and then the woman's cold, distant voice.

"*. . . pay. If you took what is mine, you will pay.*"

Jamie clicked off the tape player. She held it tightly in her lap and turned to me. "You know what this means, don't you, Lewis?"

"No. What?" I said.

"Someone was trying to contact us. Trying to connect with us. We have no choice. We have to go back there."

4

Jamie and I didn't get back to the grounds of the Fear Mansion for another week. She had the flu for a few days, and I had to go with my family to visit my cousins near Detroit.

The next Friday night, we both sneaked out of our houses a little after one in the morning and met on Fear Street. To my surprise, a lot of work had been done in the short time we were away.

The ground was still littered with roof shingles and shards of window glass. But most of the bricks from the walls, the floorboards, and the slabs of sheetrock had been hauled away.

And as Jamie and I made our way over the front yard, we saw a mountain of dirt beside a deep hole. The workers had begun to dig a foundation for the new building.

Stepping over broken shingles, we made our way to the edge of the hole and stared down. Jamie held her tape recorder in one hand. She grabbed my arm with the other hand and held on to me.

A dog barked somewhere down the street, the only other sign of life. We were surrounded by dark trees, still in a windless night.

"This mansion had such a reputation," Jamie said softly. "So many rumors and stories. And now look at it. It's just a pile of dirt and a hole in the ground."

"Did you play the tape for Christa and Elena?" I asked.

She shook her head. She had a floppy, purple cap over her hair. She wore a baggy sweater pulled down over her jeans and had a long scarf wrapped around her neck. "I was sick, remember? I told them about it, but I couldn't play it for them."

"Aaron and Whitney said they were here Wednesday night," I told Jamie. "I didn't tell them about the ghost or anything. No way they'd believe me."

"What were they doing here?" Jamie asked. She didn't wait for an answer. She let out a soft cry and dropped to her knees.

She stared into the hole. "Hey, Lewis—what's that down there?"

I squatted beside her. At first I didn't see anything. But then I saw a dull sparkle in the dirt. "Just a piece of metal, I think."

"No," she whispered, leaning into the hole. "It's a jewel. Some kind of jewel."

I squinted into the darkness. The object had a blue glow.

Jamie lowered her feet into the hole and started to slide down the side. "I've got to check it out," she said. "Look. It *is* a jewel. I think it's a pendant or a pin."

"No—wait!" I shouted. "What's *that*?" I pointed.

Something curved and pale poked up from the dirt floor of the hole. "Jamie—wait."

She saw it too. She stopped her slide, but remained perched on the edge with her feet dangling down. "Whoa, Lewis—" She let out a sharp cry. "Is it a bone?"

"I . . . think so." I poked my head over the side of the hole. A cloud rolled away from the moon. Yellow light washed over us, and suddenly the floor of the hole came into sharp focus.

And I saw bones . . .

. . . a lot of bones—ribs, maybe. Two sets, side by side. And a long arm bone poking up from under the ground. And beside the ribs, two skeletal hands, curled tightly as if gripping the dirt.

"Are they human?" Jamie asked in a tiny voice. "Human bones?"

"Yeah," I murmured. It was suddenly hard to breathe. I had to force air in and out of my lungs. "Human bones. Two skeletons, I think. Let's go, Jamie. I think we should—"

"Fears!" Jamie exclaimed. "Don't you think? Members of the Fear family who were buried beneath the house? Oh, wow. Lewis. Maybe it's Simon and Angelica Fear. Maybe it's their bones. The workmen accidentally uncovered their graves."

My chest ached. I still had trouble breathing. This was a little too creepy for me. I didn't want to admit that to Jamie. She thinks I'm some kind of macho guy because I like to climb mountains with my family and hike out in the woods for days and stuff.

But I really didn't want to be here staring at two skeletons half-buried in the dirt.

"Jamie, let's go," I said. I tried to tug her arm. But she jerked it away from me and started to slide down the dirt wall, into the hole.

"Hey—stop! What are you *doing*?" I cried, and made another grab for her.

"The jewel," she said. "It's a pendant. It . . . it's beautiful. I have to try . . ."

"No, wait—"

She started to slide fast. She flung out both arms to slow her fall. Her floppy cap caught on a twig poking out from the dirt wall and lifted off her head.

"Hey, NO—" Jamie uttered a cry as she landed hard on the bottom. Her knees gave way and she toppled forward.

I gasped as she fell on top of one of the skeletons. She landed face-down over the curving ribs. "Oh, help!" she cried, struggling to pull herself away.

Then I froze and stared in disbelief as a skeletal hand started to move. The hand slowly lifted itself from the dirt. The bony fingers uncurled—and grabbed Jamie's scarf.

"Ohhhh." A moan escaped my throat as I saw the other bony hand reach up. The hands grabbed Jamie's scarf and tugged hard.

In the bright moonlight, I saw the confused expression on Jamie's face. Saw her eyes bulge in shock. It took her a while to realize what was happening.

But I saw. I saw *everything*!

And then the skeletal hands. . . .

The hands. . . .

They wrapped around Jamie's throat.

I leaped into the hole. I flew down the wall of dirt and landed hard on my feet beside Jamie.

Pain shot up my legs. But I ignored it and grabbed the skeleton hands. I struggled to pull them off Jamie's throat. But the bony hands wrapped tightly around her neck and held on.

I couldn't budge them.

And before I could try something else, the dirt beside me shifted. I heard a sick, hollow groan, like air escaping from a balloon. And the other skeleton—bones cracking, cracking, and crackling as it moved—lifted up from the dark floor of the hole.

I felt cold, hard bony fingers tighten

around my neck. I fell to the ground, twisting and thrashing, trying to squirm away, trying to fight it off. But my whole body was heavy with panic. And I couldn't breathe . . . couldn't breathe. . . .

Beside me, I saw Jamie—eyes wide, mouth locked in a wide O of horror—being strangled . . . strangled by the skeleton, a hideous grin on the dirt-caked skull.

The strong, bony hands tightened around my throat and squeezed.

Twisting to pull free, I felt something drop onto my back. And then something hit my shoulders. I saw dirt flying . . . dirt falling into the hole. Falling on my head, my back. . . .

I couldn't breathe . . . couldn't breathe at all.

The dirt fell into the hole from above.

And over the roar, I heard that ghostly woman's voice: *"You'll pay . . . you'll ALL pay now . . ."*

The mountain of dirt was flying, flying and falling, filling up the hole again.

The two skulls grinned. The hard, bony hands tightened and squeezed.

And the dirt rained down.

My last thought: Jamie and I . . . no one will find us.

No one will ever know where we are.

We are being strangled—*and buried alive!*

PART TWO

ONE YEAR
LATER

5

Ryland O'Connor, the bartender at Nights, flashed me a thumbs-up as I stepped into the bar. "Hey, whussup, Nate?"

"Not much. The usual," I said. We bumped knuckles.

Ryland is a tall, stocky, red-faced guy with spiky blond hair, a silver ring in one ear, and crinkled-up eyes that always seem to be laughing. He has three tiny, blue stars tattooed on his right temple. And a long scar on one cheek that he won't tell anyone how he got.

He wears tight muscle shirts so everyone can see he works out. Most nights he wears torn shorts and sandals, like he's going to the beach.

Ryland is a good guy.

He knows we're high school kids, and we flash him phony IDs whenever he remembers to card us. But he doesn't care. He serves us our beers and winks about it as long as there's no trouble and kids don't start acting crazy.

Besides, the Night People are the only ones who give him an excuse to stay open all night. Everyone else in the town of Shadyside is asleep.

I stepped past the bar and glanced around, squinting in the dim, red glow of light. "Shark here yet?"

Ryland nodded. "The booth in back. With a girl."

A girl?

"Not Candy, right? Any sign of Candy?" I asked.

Ryland pulled a bottle of Coors from the bar fridge, popped the top, and handed it to me. "Which one is she? The kinda chubby one with the black curls?"

I nodded. "Yeah, that's her."

He took a sip of club soda. Ryland only drinks club soda. "Haven't seen her tonight." He grinned at me and brushed back his spiky hair. "That the one you're hot for, Nate? I thought you were into the tall one with the long blond hair. Whitney Something."

"Whitney's going out with Aaron," I said. "And no way, man. I mean about Candy. No way. Really. She's bad news. Ask Shark."

I saw Shark sitting with a blonde-haired girl in the red vinyl booth at the back wall. "Yo—Shark!" I called to him and started over there.

But Ryland called me back. "Nate, you forgot something."

"Oh. Sorry." I reached for my wallet.

"No. Not that," Ryland said. He gestured with his head to the brass plaque on the wall next to the entrance.

"Oh, yeah. I forgot." I backed up and kissed the plaque. Kissed Angelica Fear right on the lips.

The plaque shows the two original Fears, Angelica and Simon. Just their faces, young faces, like they're in their twenties or maybe thirties. Underneath the picture it says, FIRST SETTLERS OF SHADYSIDE. FEAR MANSION BUILT ON THIS SPOT IN 1889.

We all kiss the plaque when we come into Nights. I mean, just about everyone kisses it. Partly as a joke, and maybe some of us think it keeps bad luck away.

"Hey, Ryland," I said, "you ever feel funny about this?" I pointed to the plaque with my beer bottle. "I mean, this bar being right on the spot where the Fear Mansion used to stand? Does that ever creep you out?"

"Ooh, I'm scared. I'm totally scared," he said, pretending to shake. His grin faded. "Like, no way, man. I could care less about the stupid old legends and scare stories."

Ryland scratched the scar on his cheek. "Look at this place. The bar is doing business big-time. Fear Street Acres is amazing, man. I mean, the crowds are unbelievable. Talk about changing a whole part of town. Who remembers the old Fear Street? Nobody. That's ancient history."

"That's great, man," I said, glancing at the blank-eyed faces of the Fears on the plaque. Shark and Aaron and I and a few other kids spent one Halloween night in the Fear Street woods when we were in sixth grade. And I still remembered the strange howls and cries we heard coming from the Fear Mansion all night long.

We were scared that night. No kidding.

When they tore down that old house, I

expected them to find a huge pile of dead bodies inside. And I expected weird creatures and mutants and vampires and things to come flying out.

But none of that happened.

It was kinda disappointing. Just piles of bricks and shingles and broken glass, chunks of plaster, and wallboards. And a lot of old junk in a hidden room that used to belong to the Fears.

I took some cool, old photographs. And I found a belt that had a silver skull for a buckle.

Shark has a pistol he found in that room. He says Simon Fear probably killed dozens of people with it. He showed it to his dad, and his dad made him put it in a lockbox in the basement.

I glanced at the yellow neon Budweiser clock hanging on the wall behind the bar. It was a little before two in the morning.

I had to grin.

My parents are divorced, and my mom doesn't get home from work till seven every night. Sometimes she tells me I look tired and should get more rest. She doesn't have a *clue* that I have this secret night life. None of our parents do.

Yeah, we're all wrecked a lot of the time. But it's totally worth it.

I took another sip of my beer and headed to Shark's booth in back. He was busy talking to the blonde girl, spinning his beer bottle between his hands and tapping his feet. Shark is a tense guy; he's always moving.

Like a shark, I guess. Ha.

But before I got back there I heard footsteps behind me, and someone called my name.

I turned and saw Jamie Richards smiling at me. Jamie is one of the prettiest and one of the nicest girls at Shadyside High. She still walks with a slight limp from her accident last year.

I guess she's lucky to be alive.

A year ago she and her boyfriend, Lewis Baransky, were hanging out at the wreckage of the Fear Mansion late at night. And they accidentally fell into the open foundation hole. When they fell, it started a landslide of dirt, all crushing in on them.

I mean, that's what they *think* happened. Neither one of them remembers that night at all. I guess it was too terrifying, and their memory was wiped clean.

Luckily these two off-duty cops came by at

just the right time. The cops saw Jamie and Lewis fall in the hole. Somehow, they pulled them out before they were buried alive.

A miracle. They both had broken bones and things busted inside them. And psychological issues, I guess. They were both in the hospital a long time, and they didn't get to graduate with the rest of their class. I think they're really bummed to have to do twelfth grade all over again.

They both had to recuperate at home for months. Jamie said it wasn't a total waste of time. She took up sculpting with clay and found she was really good at it. Her father set up a studio with a kiln for her in the garage, and she spent most of her time there.

I think Lewis spent the time playing video games, watching the Japanese anime movies that he loves, and begging his parents to let him out of the house. He's a tall, wiry, active kinda guy, and I think he went nuts being trapped in the house for so long.

So now they're both doing okay. A few weeks ago, they started sneaking out of their houses after midnight again and meeting up with the rest of us at Nights.

"How's it going, Jamie?" I asked.

"Not bad," she said, tossing back her dark hair. "Filling out college applications. You believe I had to start all over again?"

"Weren't you accepted at Brown?"

"Yeah. But they wouldn't hold my place for a year. It was so obnoxious." She turned to Ryland. "Diet Coke?"

"Where's Lewis?" I asked.

She frowned. "I don't think he's coming tonight. He's been kinda messed up."

"Messed up? You mean sick?"

She shook her head. "No. Nightmares. Lewis has these weird nightmares. He gets totally creeped out by them, then he can't sleep." She sighed. "He still dreams about the accident. We both do. I . . . I just can't put it behind me."

"Sorry," I said. I didn't know what else to say. I really liked Jamie. I guess I had a crush on her. But she and Lewis had been going together since junior high or something. No way I stood a chance there.

She took her Diet Coke from Ryland, and I led the way to the back. "Who's that girl with Shark?" I asked her. "Ever see her before?"

Shark and the girl were laughing about something. The girl had her back to us. All we could see was her streaked, white-blonde hair down over the collar of her red sweater. Then she turned and we could see her face.

She had straight bangs across her forehead, high cheekbones like a magazine model, and big, round green eyes. A *babe*!

"Oh, yeah. I know her," Jamie said. "Nikki Howitz. She's friends with Ada, but she doesn't go to Shadyside. She goes to Waynesbridge."

We stepped up to their booth. "Hey, whussup?" Shark said. He and I slapped a high five. He gave Jamie a two-fingered salute.

"Move it," I said, dropping into the booth and shoving Shark over. I kept sliding in until there was room for Jamie. Shark introduced Nikki.

"What was so funny?" I asked.

"Your face," Shark replied.

"Shut up," Nikki said. "You guys are friends, right?"

"Nate is my friend, but I'm not his friend," Shark said. He giggled. Like that was so funny.

"Don't pay any attention to him," Nikki said. "Ask him how many beers he's drunk."

Shark's eyes *did* look a little funny. Like they were floating around loose in his head. I squinted at him. "What's your problem, man?"

A sly smile spread over his face. "Do I need a problem?" he tilted his beer bottle at me in a salute, then took a long pull.

"You're friends with Ada, right?" Jamie said to Nikki.

"Shut up. How'd you know that?" Nikki replied.

"She talks about you sometimes," Jamie said. "You're a swimmer, right? All-state or something."

Nikki grinned at her. "You know everything about me."

"Ada and I were counselors at the same camp," Jamie said. "Camp Running Cloud? We hung out a lot. Really got to know each other."

Shark slid his arm around Nikki's shoulders. "Nikki and I are going camping," he said. "Just the two of us."

She gave him a hard shove. "In your dreams."

Shark laughed. He turned to me with a wide grin on his face. "Know what I did to

Candy Shutt tonight? You gotta hear this."

Jamie narrowed her eyes at Shark. "What you *did* to her?"

Shark nodded. "She's trying to get back with me, do you believe it?"

"Huh?" I exclaimed. "But *she* dumped *you.*"

"Yeah, yeah." Shark's grin faded. "That's old news."

Candy really messed Shark up last year. I mean, he was totally into her. And then she lied and said she had the flu, and he saw her that night making out like crazy with Andy Johnson in the backseat of Andy's car.

Shark was, like, blown away by that. I mean, totally hurt. Of course he never let on. And he never said anything to me.

You've gotta read between the lines with Shark. You have to know him as well as I do, or else you'll never be able to read him. Because he never lets on.

But he did some wild things after that night. He'd get really tanked at Nights, and then he'd go out and pull up mailboxes and break some windows. And he stole a car and drove it around all night. Then he returned it before the owner woke up in the morning.

He's a good guy. But he can go a little nuts.

I'm the calm one. Everyone says, "Nate is low-key, not temperamental." Sometimes I try to tell Shark to take a breath. You know, count to ten. But how do you hold back a *shark?*

"Okay, spill," I said. "What did you do to Candy Shutt?"

6

"She came to Nights last night," Shark said, spinning the beer bottle between his hands. "By the way, Nate, where were you?"

"I did Calculus problems till two a.m.," I said. "I can't believe Martin assigned half the textbook!"

"Well, anyway, I was waiting for Nikki, and Candy came striding in. You know the way she walks. Like she owns the place. Like she's a star or something. And she cornered me in that booth over there." He pointed.

"Then she totally came on to me. She kept kissing me and, like, breathing on me, and saying we should take a walk together. And how she missed me so much it hurt."

Nikki's green eyes went wide. "Shut up. I don't believe it. Just before I came in?"

Shark nodded. "Yeah. She was, like, all over me, man. She said we were so right together. So good together. You know. Like out of some wacked-out romance novel."

Shark shook his head and laughed. Then he raised the beer bottle to his mouth and emptied it.

"So what did you do?" Jamie asked him.

Shark let out a loud burp.

"Can't take him anywhere," Nikki muttered. "You're so gross."

Shark grabbed my arm. He grinned at me. "Know what I did, Nate? I told her I felt the same way about her."

"Shut up!" Nikki cried. She gave Shark a hard shove.

Shark ignored her. "I said I couldn't wait to hook up with her. I said I'd meet her tonight. Go to a movie. I told her to meet me at nine at the Cineplex."

"Get out!" Nikki said. "Did you go?"

"Of course not," Shark said. "*No way* I'd go out with that slut."

"You stood her up?" Jamie asked. "She was waiting there at nine, and you just didn't show up?"

Shark nodded, still grinning. "Yeah."

"Why didn't you just tell her to take a walk?" Jamie asked.

"This was funnier," Shark said.

"But—," Jamie started.

"And think how good she felt all day," Shark said. "Thinking she was going out with me. It made her day, right? I mean, till nine o'clock."

"That's mean," Jamie said.

"For sure," Shark agreed, his eyes flashing. "And then here's what else I did. I changed the voicemail message on my cell. I changed it to say, 'Have a nice day, Candy, you slut.'"

Shark took my beer from my hand and finished it. "And sure enough, about nine twenty, my cell rang. I recognized Candy's number. I didn't pick up so she'd get my special message." He tossed back his head and laughed.

I just stared at him and didn't say a word. I didn't know what to say. I knew Shark was kinda wild and liked to act like a macho guy. But I never knew he had such a mean streak.

I guess Candy had hurt him more than we realized.

Shark was still laughing when Jamie suddenly waved her hands for him to be quiet. Jamie's eyes were on the front door.

We all turned and saw the figure sweeping toward us.

Candy Shutt.

My heart started to pound. "Look out, dude," I told Shark. "Here she comes. And no joke—she looks like she could murder some-one."

7

Candy didn't stop to kiss the brass plaque on the wall. She came roaring down the bar like a charging elephant.

She was big and red-faced. Her jaw was clenched, and she had her hands balled into fists. She wore a pale blue top and a short black skirt, very tight, over dark blue tights. Her curly black hair bounced on her head as she trod up to us.

"I'm out of here," Jamie said, jumping to her feet. "I hate violence."

"Me too," I said. I wanted to join Jamie, but I couldn't scramble out of the booth fast enough.

Jamie took one step and Candy bulled right into her.

"Oh!" both girls cried out.

Candy bounced back, breathing hard. Her tiny, black eyes went wide. "Look out," she growled.

Jamie lowered her eyes to Candy's shirt. "What's that?" she asked, pointing.

The question took Candy by surprise. She followed Jamie's gaze. "My pendant?"

Jamie nodded. She wrapped her fingers around it. "Are these real jewels?"

"I don't know," Candy said. She glanced at Shark, and her face turned red again. "I think so."

"It looks like it's really old," Jamie said.

She lowered her head to examine the silver pendant closely. I couldn't tell if she was really interested in it, or if she was just trying to distract Candy and keep her from murdering Shark.

"Weird," Jamie murmured, eyeing the blue jewels. "I just had this strange flash. Like I'd seen this pendant before."

"Yeah. Weird," Candy said. She scowled at Shark.

"Where'd you get it?" Jamie asked.

Candy let out an impatient sigh. "At a store, okay?" She still had her hands knotted into tight fists. She really wanted to get to Shark.

But Jamie wouldn't let her get by. "What store?" she asked. "Around here?"

"That little jewelry store. The Fear Street Gold Mine. Okay? Right across the street from this bar. I saw it in the window."

"Oh. Wow . . ." Jamie ran her fingers over the pendant's silver clasp. "Very pretty. Thanks for letting me see it. Bye, guys. I've got to go home now."

Jamie edged past Candy and made her way, limping, to the front door.

I saw Candy take a deep breath, as if gathering back her anger. Then she spun on Shark.

"You—you lying piece of . . ." With an angry cry, she threw herself over the table, swinging her fists at him.

I pinned myself against the back of the booth to get out of the way. Shark laughed and dodged her punches.

Screaming at the top of her lungs, Candy let out a string of curses. Nikki went pale and tried to duck away. With a deafening shriek of fury, Candy picked up Shark's beer bottle and turned it over his head.

Empty.

Shark laughed.

Candy tossed the bottle at him. He ducked, and the bottle bounced off the back of the padded booth and clattered onto the table-top.

"Give it up, Candy," I said. "Take a breath."

I don't think she heard me. She was still screaming and cursing.

I scrambled out of the booth. This was kinda scary. She was totally out of control. I saw the worried look on Nikki's face. Shark was the only one smiling.

And then, with a shrill cry, Candy threw herself over the table again. She grabbed Shark by the shoulders and jerked him forward.

Their faces met. Candy pushed her mouth against his.

Shark uttered a startled gasp.

Grunting angrily, Candy pressed her mouth hard against Shark's lips. She gripped him tightly. I saw him struggle to free himself.

But she held him there, groaning, grinding her mouth against his.

"Candy, let go——," I said. I started toward her.

With a cry, she ended the horrifying kiss and backed away. Her dark eyes were glowing. Her mouth twisted in an awful grin.

I saw Shark's eyes go wide. And then he opened his mouth in a scream.

Bright red blood poured down his chin. His lips—they were open. Cut open and gushing blood.

Candy tossed back her head and laughed. And I saw Shark's blood on her teeth and lips, running down her chin.

"BIT me. . . ." Shark groaned. His lips were totally ripped open and swelling up. The blood rolled down his chin onto the front of his T-shirt. "She bit me. . . ."

8

Jamie had watched the whole thing from the front door. Now she came hurrying back to us. I looked for Ryland, but I didn't see him.

"Shark . . . he's totally cut up," Jamie said. "I have my car. We'd better get him to the hospital."

"No hospital!" Shark screamed. He covered his lips with both hands.

Candy laughed again. Her face was bright red, and her dark eyes flashed with excitement. "Bye, everyone," she shouted, using the back of her hand to wipe the blood from her lips.

She turned to leave, but Nikki leaped up from the table and grabbed her by the shoulders. "How could you do that?" Nikki screamed. "How could you *do* that to him?"

"Let go of me," Candy said, lowering her voice. She suddenly seemed calm. She narrowed her eyes, locking them on Nikki. "Let go of me, slut. I'll tear you to pieces. I mean it. I'll tear you apart."

She said it so coldly, so intently, Nikki's mouth dropped open and she backed away.

Candy spun around, shoved Jamie out of her way, and stomped heavily to the front door.

Jamie turned to Shark. She grabbed his arm. "You need stitches. We have to get you to the hospital."

Shark didn't answer. He stared straight ahead, one hand still pressed over his mouth. I could see the anger in his eyes. I'd seen Shark angry before, but not like this. I almost expected to see steam spouting from his head.

Nikki's face was pale. Her chin quivered. "Shark?" she called to him softly. "Shark? Are you okay? Can you hear us? Jamie thinks—"

Shark tore out of the booth. "Grab those beer bottles," he said. He was breathing noisily. His eyes were wild.

"Shark?" I said. "What are you doing?"

I don't know why I obeyed him. I guess it

was just a habit. I grabbed the two bottles and followed him, running out of the bar. I glanced back and saw Nikki and Jamie hurrying after us.

We burst out of the bar in time to see Candy's car pull away. She drove a little red BMW, an early graduation gift from her parents.

The tires squealed as Candy gunned the engine, and the car took off, barreling down Fear Street.

"Shark, *don't!*" Nikki shrieked.

But Shark grabbed a bottle from my hands. He took a running start, pulled back his arm, and heaved it at the back of the little BMW.

I let out a cry as the bottle missed its target and shattered noisily on the pavement.

Then, without thinking, I took my turn.

Why did I fling the second bottle at Candy's car? I'm always the sensible one, always the one trying to cool Shark down.

Maybe I'd had too much beer. Or maybe it was the sight of Shark's bleeding, torn mouth. I felt so angry!

I took a running start and threw the bottle with all my strength. And a second later, I heard the crash—the sound of shattering glass.

Shark and the others cheered. Someone slapped me on the back. "Way to go, Nate!"

The car squealed to a stop.

It took me a moment to realize Candy's car was backing up. I heard the roar of the engine first. The squeal of tires. Then the car came shooting toward us, swerving wildly this way and that.

"Look out—!" I screamed. I leaped onto the sidewalk and pressed my back against the front of the bar.

Shark jumped the other way. He lowered his body and dove as the back end of the car bulleted toward him. *"You crazy idiot!"* he screamed at Candy.

The car squealed to a stop, tires scraping the pavement.

"I'll pay you back," she shouted. Her hoarse scream rang out through the shattered rear window. "You'll pay! I mean it!"

Was she shouting at Shark—or at me? Did she see that I was the one who smashed her car window?

No one moved. We stood and watched as Candy angrily shifted gears and the tires squealed again as the little car started to pull away.

"You'll pay!" Candy screamed again over the roar of the engine. "You'll ALL pay!"

The words sent a chill down my back.

I froze as Candy's warning repeated and repeated in my mind.

"You'll pay. You'll *all* pay. . . ."

PART THREE

9

A week after I broke Candy's car window, the weather changed, and the air started to feel wintry cold. The clouds hung low, gray, and gloomy.

Shark's mouth was still swollen. He looked like he had a duck beak or something. His lips were all black and scabby, but he said it was healing okay.

He was still raging about Candy. "I could have her arrested," he said as we walked to my house after school. "That was assault. A definite assault. Look at this. I had six stitches."

His big lips formed a lopsided grin. "Think she'd like that, Nate? Think Candy would like having a police record? That would look good on her application to NYU, wouldn't it?"

"But you can't do it, man," I said. "If you

turned her in, everyone would find out when it happened. We'd be totally busted. Everyone would find out that we all sneak out at night."

Shark frowned. "Think I don't know it? But, man, I'd love to get her. You believe this? Every time I pass her in the hall at school she turns away. Like *she's* the hurt one."

He pounded his fist into a corner mailbox. "First she dumps me. Then she practically rips my mouth off. And *she's* the one who's hurt."

I hated when Shark went into these rages. Sometimes he'd go ballistic for hours. It was really scary.

He was a big, strong guy, very athletic. If he wanted to, he could really hurt someone. He was my best buddy, and I knew he was a really good friend. But, whoa—I was afraid of his temper.

Not so much for myself. I was afraid of the trouble he might get into if he ever *really* lost it.

I unlocked the kitchen door, and we went into the house. No one was home.

We grabbed Cokes and a bag of tortilla chips and went up to my room. We played Grand Theft Auto—the original game—on my PlayStation for a while.

Shark's cell rang. It was Nikki. He talked to her for a while. She said she might sneak out and come to Nights tonight.

I had a chem final the next morning. I didn't plan to go out tonight. I planned to cram for the test until I dropped. But you never know . . . sometimes I'm already in bed, and I wake up at one or two. And the urge hits me. No way I can stay in bed. I think, I've *got* to go out and see what's up with everyone at Nights.

We played the video game a little more, and then *my* cell rang. It was Mom telling me she wouldn't be home till late. I had to get my own dinner. I asked her what she was doing, and she got kinda giggly and weird. Finally she said she was going out on a date.

Cute, right?

I'm sixteen and I don't go out on dates. Nobody I know goes out on dates. We all pretty much just hang out.

And my *mom* is going out on a date.

It made me feel a little weird.

I suddenly thought about my dad. He moved away from Shadyside after the divorce. Now he lives in an apartment on the ocean in

Santa Barbara. Man, it's beautiful there. I visited him twice, and I didn't want to leave.

I suddenly wondered if *he* was going out on dates.

Whenever I think about Mom and Dad, and how it used to be when we all lived together, and how it is now, with them not speaking and all . . . well . . . it makes me feel kinda sick to my stomach.

Shark and I pulled chairs over to my computer, and we went online. We like to go to this one Web site called meetup-place.com. It's a big chat room with guys and girls meeting up and coming on to each other. And mainly telling lies.

I got into this conversation with someone named Wildgirl345. My screen name is Straydog.

> *Wildgirl345: What do U like to do, Straydog?*
>
> *Straydog: I'll do anything once. Especially with you. lol*
>
> *Wildgirl345: U sound hot. What do you look like?*
>
> *Straydog: People say I'm like a young Brad Pitt.*

Wildgirl345: Ooh, I HATE Brad Pitt.

Straydog: Yeah. Me too. He totally sucks. I don't know y people say that about me. I don't look anything like him!

Wildgirl345: How old r u, Straydog?

Straydog: I was 22 last week.

Wildgirl345: Hey, that's neat. I'm 22 too!

See? Shark and I loved to go on this Web site and tell lies. Of course, Wildgirl345 was lying too. She was probably fourteen. She said she lived in a penthouse in New York City and she was a fashion model.

Yeah. For sure.

That's when I signed off. Shark signed on. His screen name is Shark. Clever, huh? He started talking up three girls at once. It was starting to get pretty hot, when Shark was interrupted:

Hey, Big Lips—it's pay up time.

The message came from Candylishus.

Shark groaned. "It's Candy."

He didn't type anything back. Just scowled at the screen.

But Candy had more to say:

Pretty Mouth, I told my dad the car got busted when I went shopping at the mall. But you have to pay for the window. It cost $320.

Shark groaned again. He turned to me. "She thinks I broke her window. Believe it?"

"Guess she didn't see me," I said.

Shark typed back to her:

Pay for what? I don't know what you're talking about.

A few seconds later, Candy replied:

Read my lips, Big Mouth. You pay for the window. You bring me the $320 by Friday. Or I'll have no choice. Ever hear the expression "The truth hurts"? I'll tell my dad the truth. I'll tell him about the Night People.

Shark was sitting in my desk chair. I was leaning over his shoulder. We both stared at the screen.

I could see Shark's whole body tighten. His jaw clenched. He got really tense.

I suddenly felt cold all over. Was she serious?

No way you can do that. You'll ruin it for everyone.

Candy wrote back:

>*Duh. That's kinda the point, Brain.*
>*I'm totally serious here. Pay up, or you'll*
>*ALL be busted.*

Shark slammed his hand on the desk. He typed:

>*You'll be busted too.*

Candy's reply:

>*Think my dad cares what I do?*
>*That's a joke. He only cares about the*
>*window on the BMW.*

Shark swept his hand back over his spiky hair. His jaw was still clenched tight. He stared at the screen. "I don't believe it," he whispered.

>*Your parents will be thrilled when*
>*they find out. And how about our good*
>*school principal? Wow. You could all be*
>*suspended. What a shame that would be,*
>*huh? All those seniors suspended.*

Shark turned to me, his face red with anger. "I'm going to kill her," he said.

"That's way too good for her," I said. I started pacing back and forth. I realized I was clenching and unclenching my fists.

I wanted to kill Candy too. I mean, if my mom found out I've been sneaking out to a bar with my buddies every night at two in the morning, she . . . she . . . I don't know what she'd do. She'd be so hurt and disappointed.

I never thought about my mom finding out. Honest. I never thought about it till Candy's threat.

Shark hadn't moved. He sat there, staring at the screen as a final message popped up from Candy:

Bring the $$$ to school. c u then.

Have a lovely day! :)

Shark let out an angry cry. He jumped to his feet and turned to me. "What am I going to do about her, Nate? I mean, what am I going to *do*?"

10

We paid Candy. We had no choice. We couldn't let her rat us out and ruin our lives. So Shark and I scraped up the money. We each paid half.

Shark handed it to her in homeroom. She didn't say a word to him. Just grinned as if she'd won some kind of big victory.

Shark's face turned bright red with anger when Candy grinned at him like that. I suddenly had a heavy feeling in my stomach. I knew he wasn't finished with her.

A few days later he came over to my house again. We went up to my room and started messing around on the computer.

Shark double-clicked the Photoshop icon and started clicking and typing furiously. The doorbell rang, and I ran downstairs to answer it.

It was just a package for my mom from UPS. When I returned to my room, Shark was still hunched over the keyboard, working intently.

I gazed at the monitor. "Hey, what is that?"

A grin spread over his face. "Check this out, dude."

I leaned closer to the screen. It took me a few seconds to recognize it—the senior class Web site. It's the site where they post homework assignments, news and announcements, special dates to remember—junk like that.

"It's the class Web site," I said. "So?"

Shark's grin grew wider. "I found a way to hack into it."

"You mean . . . ?"

"Watch," he said. He typed some more, then clicked a few things with his mouse.

A color photo appeared in the *Class News Bulletin* section. A photo of a humungous hog.

"What's up with the hog?" I asked.

Shark had his eyes on the screen. "It won a prize at the Shadyside Fair last month."

"Big whoop," I said, rolling my eyes. "I didn't know you were into hogs, Shark."

"Just shut up and watch," he said. He

clicked some more, sliding the mouse rapidly, concentrating hard.

He changed the photo. Candy's face replaced the hog's face. It was Candy's yearbook photo.

I stared at it for a few seconds. Candy's face on the huge, gross hog. And then I burst out laughing.

It was totally perfect. Awesome!

"I'm not finished," Shark said. He typed in a caption. He changed one letter in Candy's last name. He changed her name from Shutt to Slutt.

And then he wrote a short paragraph under the photo:

NEWS BULLETIN

Candy Slutt may miss second semester because she's expecting a litter of baby hogs.

He moved the photo and caption over to the news section of the Web site. It really looked like part of the senior news page.

Shark and I both laughed. It was a riot.

"You're not going to send it, are you?" I asked. "I mean, no one else will see it?"

He narrowed his eyes at me. "You're kidding, right? *Everyone* will see it, Nate. I told you. I hacked into the Web site."

"But . . . you could get in major trouble," I said. "Change it back, man. I mean, really. Change it back. If Mr. Gonzalez finds out. Or what's-his-name, that new vice-principal—"

"They won't know who did it," Shark said.

"But Candy will know who did it," I said. "Candy will know, and—"

"So what?" Shark replied. He shrugged "So *what* if Candy knows? What could happen?"

11

Shark's little hog joke worked better than he ever imagined.

I was at my locker on Monday morning when Candy arrived at school. I heard the kids oinking behind her back. She pretended not to hear it, but I saw her face turn bright red and her mouth tighten in a tense scowl.

"Oink. Oink."

"Runnnnk runnnk."

Guys made hog sounds when Candy walked past. People giggled. And I heard some girls whispering about "Candy *Slutt*" and laughing. Of course, they stopped when Candy came close to them.

But I knew that Candy heard them. You just had to look at Candy's face. I mean, she was ready to explode.

She stopped me in the hall as I was walking into homeroom. She pushed me hard by the shoulders, backing me against the tile wall.

"Shark did it—didn't he?" she asked through gritted teeth. Her breath smelled like bacon. No kidding. I almost burst out laughing. I guess she had bacon and eggs or something for breakfast.

But I pictured that gross hog photo, so totally fat with Candy's round, smiling face on it. And there she was, smelling like bacon. And I almost totally lost it.

She shoved me against the wall again. "Tell the truth, Nate," she growled. "It was Shark, right? He's the computer whiz around here. I know it."

I shrugged and tried to keep a straight face. "I don't know," I said. "Really."

Some kid down the hall oinked. I heard some other guys laughing.

Candy let out an angry cry. She had me backed against the wall. I couldn't get away. "I . . . don't get it," she said. Her voice broke. "Why does he hate me so much? I . . . I . . ."

"Maybe because you dumped him," I said. I had to say something. I didn't want her to go ballistic. I couldn't forget the night she nearly bit Shark's lips off!

"Maybe you really hurt him," I said.

Her tiny, dark eyes narrowed to slits. "He's just a vicious jerk," she whispered.

"Oink. Oinnnnk." Someone inside the classroom.

Candy spun away from me. I slid away from the wall. The bell rang, loud, right over our heads.

I hurried into the room. I didn't see where she went. She didn't show up in homeroom.

I guess she had a really hard time all day. I heard kids oinking and making hog sounds and calling, "Slutt Slutt Slutt!" all day.

Shark was very pleased with himself. "Everyone saw it on the Web site," he told me, his eyes flashing happily. "It's, like, that's how she'll always be remembered. Maybe they'll even put it in the yearbook." He laughed and slapped me a hard high five.

But I didn't really feel like laughing. I mean, it was pretty funny. But was it worth it?

As it turned out—no.

It all boiled over the next day.

12

"Shut up! That's totally mean!" Nikki declared.

"It was a riot," Shark insisted.

Nikki shook her head. "But that poor girl—"

"She deserved it," Shark said. He took a long pull on his bottle of beer. "Hey, Nate—did she deserve it or what?"

I shrugged.

I kinda agreed with Nikki. I couldn't believe it myself—but I was starting to feel a little sorry for Candy. Well . . . maybe not *sorry*.

I guess I just didn't want the whole thing to explode in our faces. I didn't want our whole senior year wrecked because of a stupid prank.

Shark's hog photo had been a joke. But this morning, Candy had been humiliated in front of everyone at Shadyside High.

And now it was late that night, about two in the morning. Shark, Nikki, and I were sitting in our back booth at Nights and talking about what had gone down in the auditorium.

You see, there had been an assembly this morning instead of first period. Some guy from the Green Party came to speak about how he wanted to save the trees in the Fear Street Woods. The woods started at the end of Fear Street and stretched for miles.

But a lot of trees had been torn down when they built the Fear Street Acres shopping center. And this guy wanted to make sure the rest of the woods were left alone.

Well, wouldn't you know it? Mr. Gonzalez chose Candy to introduce the speaker. I guess because Candy had circulated some kind of petition about saving the trees when school started in September.

So Candy was sitting onstage with Mr. Gonzalez and the speaker, who was young and kinda cool looking. He was dressed all in black and had a shiny earring in one ear and tattoos of birds on the backs of both hands.

Gonzalez said a few things and told us to be a good audience and to show that Shadyside High really cares. You know. He was really telling us to shut up and pretend to listen to this guy.

Then he introduced Candy. And Candy got up from her chair. She had a speech all prepared. I saw she was holding it in one hand.

Shark and I were sitting with our friend Galen on an aisle near the back of the auditorium. Lewis and Jamie sat in front of us. I knew that Lewis was really into saving the woods because he and his family go camping there a lot. At least they did before his accident.

Candy stepped up to the podium and cleared her throat. And Galen started to oink really loudly.

That got a pretty good laugh.

Candy looked kinda flustered. She just stood there.

Then some other guys at the side of the auditorium oinked. And someone went "Runnk runnnk" and really sounded like a hog. And now everyone was laughing.

Almost immediately, more guys started oinking. I mean, the hog sounds were, like, echoing off the auditorium walls.

Shark touched knuckles with Galen and me, and he joined in, oinking at the top of his lungs.

Mr. Gonzalez jumped to his feet. I saw the angry expression on his face. He started to the podium. But that didn't stop the oinking and hog sounds. They got even louder.

And then someone tossed a pink stuffed pig onto the stage. It bounced off the podium and landed at Candy's feet. The place went wild, everyone oinking and laughing and busting a gut.

Even from the back of the auditorium, I could see that Candy's face was bright red. Her hands were balled into tight fists at her sides.

She let out a furious cry that boomed through the loudspeakers. She began to sob. Tears rolled down her cheeks. She spun away from the podium and ran off the stage, howling and sobbing.

The laughter stopped. The oinking stopped with it. A hush fell over the auditorium. Mr.

Gonzalez stood at the podium facing the guest speaker. Neither one of them moved.

I turned to Shark. "She's going to get us," I whispered. "It went too far. She's going to get us."

13

Oinkapalooza.

That's what Shark called it. I thought that was pretty funny. But I couldn't laugh at it.

The next day I still had a heavy feeling in the pit of my stomach, a feeling that we had gone too far.

And I was right.

Mr. Grant, the new vice principal, was waiting for me outside the lunchroom that afternoon. He was a tiny, short man with slicked-back brown hair and square, rimless glasses. He wore the same gray suit to school every day.

He put a hand on my shoulder to stop me. "Nate, could you come with me to Mr. Gonzalez's office?" He had a grim expression on his face, and his tiny, gray eyes behind the square glasses stared at me intently.

He kept his hand on my shoulder the whole way to Gonzalez's office. Like maybe he thought I'd try to escape or something.

When I stepped into the principal's office, I couldn't help it—I gasped. Candy sat there with her hands clasped tightly in her lap. Her parents sat on folding chairs beside her. They all glared at me coldly.

An older man in a brown suit stood near the window. He had a writing pad in one hand. He glanced at me quickly, then scribbled something on his pad.

Mr. Gonzalez stood up and motioned me to the empty armchair beside the desk. "Nate, that's Mr. Ambrose," he said. "He's the Shutt family's attorney."

"Attorney?" My voice cracked. Totally embarrassing. My heart started to pound. "What's going on?" I asked, trying to sound calm and innocent.

Mr. Gonzalez motioned again for me to sit down. So I lowered myself into the big, green leather chair. My hands were suddenly shaking. I gripped the chair arms to cover it up.

"Nate, I'm sure you know why we're

here," Gonzalez said softly, his eyes locked on me. "The hog photo—it was traced to your computer."

I swallowed. "But—," I started.

My mouth suddenly felt dry. My stomach rolled over. I thought I might heave.

I'd started to say that it was my computer, but Shark did the photo.

But I couldn't do that. I couldn't rat out Shark.

I stared at the glittering pendant around Candy's neck. Thinking hard. Trying to decide what to do. Should I try to deny the whole thing?

"I . . . don't understand that," I said in a trembling voice. I knew they could see my hands shaking. I'm such a bad liar.

"There's no mistake," Gonzalez said. "It was traced to your computer."

"But—"

"Candy and her parents are very upset, as you can see," Gonzalez said. "They feel that you have slandered Candy and embarrassed her in a cruel and humiliating way. They are prepared to take legal action, Nate."

"But—I . . ."

I couldn't speak. A hush fell over the room. They were waiting for me to say something.

To my surprise, Candy broke the silence. "I didn't think it was you," she said. "I don't understand, Nate. Were you just showing off for Shark? Did he put you up to it?"

"N-no," I stammered. I could feel my face burning.

I'm going to have to take the heat, I decided. I can't squeal on Shark. I let him do it on my computer. I'm partly to blame anyway.

"Maybe we should call your mother," Gonzalez said.

"No. Please," I begged. "I'm really sorry. It was just a joke. It wasn't supposed to go that far. I'm really sorry. Please don't call my mother. If there's anything I can do . . ."

"You've ruined my life, Nate!" Candy screamed.

Her dad grabbed her shoulder. "Your life isn't ruined," he said. "It was a cruel joke, Candy. But everyone will forget it in a day or two."

Candy scowled at me. She fingered the jeweled pendant.

The lawyer leaned against the window ledge and scribbled on his pad.

"My wife and I don't want to make a big deal of this," Mr. Shutt told Gonzalez. "We came in because Candy is very upset. But she'll calm down."

"No, I won't!" Candy cried, glaring at me. "I won't! You don't care what happens to me. You don't care at all!"

"We know Nate's mother," Mr. Shutt continued. "We know she's gone through a hard time. We don't want Nate suspended or anything. We really want to end this and forget about it."

I let out a sigh. I couldn't believe Candy's dad was being so cool about this.

"Maybe if Nate apologizes to Candy," Mr. Shutt said. "In front of the whole school . . . ?"

"That's not enough!" Candy snapped.

"I appreciate your suggestion," Gonzalez told Mr. Shutt. "And I appreciate your thoughtfulness toward Nate." He turned to me. "Your joke was cruel and obscene, Nate."

I hung my head. "I know. I'm very sorry," I said.

But I felt really good. I was getting off the

hook. I wasn't going to be suspended. My mom wouldn't have to know.

"Yes, Nate will apologize to Candy over the loudspeaker to the entire school," Gonzalez told her parents. "Nate, I want you to write a long and sincere apology."

Candy gripped her pendant and scowled furiously at me. "That's not enough!" she shrieked again. "Not enough! Not enough!"

14

I stood next to the table, leaned in, and shouted over the jukebox. "So Mr. Shutt was this totally cool guy. He got me off the hook with Gonzalez. It was unbelievable."

Jamie shook her head. Lewis's eyes were wide with shock. "I can't believe he did that," he said. "We all thought you were dead meat."

I glanced to the back booth. Shark was there with Nikki and Galen. "I can't believe he did it either," I said. "How did such a good guy get such a loser for a daughter?"

Lewis took a long slug of his Coors. "Now what?"

I grinned. "Shark owes me big time. He can't believe I took the heat for him. Now Candy hates *me* as much as she hates Shark."

I glanced to the front. Ryland sat on a stool

watching an old Frankenstein movie on the TV above the bar.

What a long day! When I got out of Gonzalez's office, I was drenched with sweat and shaking all over. I knew I should be home asleep. But I was too wired to sleep. As soon as I knew my mom was tucked in bed, I slipped out of my bedroom window and hurried to Nights.

I gave Jamie and Lewis a wave and started back to Shark's table. Nikki was holding her wrist up to Galen, showing off a gold bracelet. I guessed it was the bracelet she'd found at the Fear Mansion.

It suddenly got noisy in the bar. Ryland's TV was blaring, and Shark and Galen and Nikki burst out laughing about something. I didn't hear Candy come into the bar.

But when I started to drop into the booth next to Galen, I saw her kiss the plaque on the wall, then come storming toward us, black hair bobbing on her head, fists swinging at her sides.

"Nate!" She shouted my name as if it was a dirty word.

My heart stopped beating for a moment. I realized I was holding my breath.

I crossed my arms in front of me and

watched Candy approach. She wore a bright red turtleneck pulled down over low-riding gray slacks. The silver pendant on a chain over her sweater caught the light, the blue jewels glowing brightly.

She strode up to the table, her eyes narrowed at me. She bumped the table hard and opened her mouth as if to speak. But she didn't say anything. Just glared at me. Too angry to speak, I guess.

"Hey, Candy. How's it going?" Shark broke the silence.

But Candy ignored him and kept her eyes on me.

Finally I found my voice. "Uh . . . sorry. You know. You accept my apology, right?" I tried to keep a straight face. She knew I wasn't too sincere.

Candy didn't answer. She stood there breathing hard, holding her fists at her sides. I think she wanted me to know that she was still furious at me. Finally she turned and started to walk away.

I expected her to leave the bar. But instead she dropped into a booth against the wall, propped her elbows on the table, rested her head in her hands, and called for Ryland to bring her a Coors Light.

The four of us tried to talk and hang out as usual. But it was hard with Candy sitting so close, glaring at us the whole time.

Shark called for another round of beers for everyone. Lewis waved good night and headed out of the bar. Jamie joined us in the back booth. She started talking about a college she'd visited in Ohio.

I kept glancing over Jamie's shoulder. Candy didn't move. Even when she sipped her beer, she had her eyes locked on me. And she was muttering, moving her lips. Like she was putting a hex on me or something.

Ryland brought the beers and a couple of bowls of beer nuts. I grabbed a handful and tossed them into my mouth. Shark started talking about the trouble he's been having with Ms. Harvey, our government teacher.

But I uttered a loud gasp, interrupting him. "Something funny about this beer nut," I said. I reached into my mouth and pulled it off my tongue.

"Whoa!" I watched it wriggle between my fingers.

A cockroach.

"Yuck." I tossed it to the floor. I grabbed my beer bottle and took a long slug.

I examined the bowl of beer nuts. Nothing moving in there.

"That was totally gross," I said. "I can still feel it crawling on my tongue."

Galen laughed. "Dude—was it crunchy?"

I started to answer, then stopped. My tongue prickled. I reached into my mouth again—and pulled out another cockroach.

The insect dropped from my fingers and scrabbled across the table.

My mouth dropped open and I started to gag. Then I felt a cockroach slither out over my lips and cling to my chin.

I grabbed Shark's arm. "I . . . don't understand . . ." I choked out.

But I couldn't talk. I pulled another cockroach off my tongue. Then another one. I tossed them to the floor. My tongue itched and throbbed. I could feel more insects crawling in my mouth—on the roof of my mouth, under my tongue, poking out through my lips.

"Whoa!" I spat the cockroaches out. One

of them flew onto the table. Another bug stuck to my cheek.

I gagged again. I pulled two more cockroaches from my open mouth. Another one slid down my chin.

My face itched. My whole body started to itch.

I struggled to keep my dinner down.

Another brown insect scrabbled out of my mouth.

"What is *happening?*" I choked out.

Cockroaches swarmed over our table.

I leaped to my feet. I shoved Galen out of the way. I pressed my hand over my mouth, squeezed out of the booth, and started running to the front door.

Where was I going? I didn't know. I couldn't think straight. Cockroaches were *pouring* out of my mouth.

"Wait! Nate—," I heard Shark calling to me.

"What's up?" Ryland called.

I couldn't answer. Cockroaches crawled over my hand. My mouth was filling up with them.

As I reached the door, I glanced back.

And saw Candy, watching me from her booth. She sat stiffly, one hand on that jeweled pendant.

And she had the biggest smile on her face.

15

"Let's cut Ms. Harvey's class," Shark said. He tossed his government text into the locker and pulled out his jacket.

I said okay. It was the last class of the day, and she was just reviewing stuff anyway.

I couldn't concentrate on anything all day. I kept thinking about the night before. Seeing cockroaches everywhere I looked.

I couldn't eat. I couldn't even *think* about putting something in my mouth.

The cockroaches didn't stop coming until I left the bar. I threw up a dozen of them into the curb on Fear Street. I hunched over the curb, feeling sick, waiting for more bugs to crawl out.

But there were no more.

The next morning my tongue kept tingling

and itching like crazy. I could feel the little legs crawling over it. I kept poking my fingers inside my mouth, feeling for more bugs. But there was nothing there.

Just the memory of it.

And the memory of Candy Shutt's strange smile. As if she was really enjoying seeing me suffer.

Shark and I stepped out the back door by the boys' locker room. It was a warm day, the sun beaming down in a cloudless sky. I unzipped my jacket. It felt more like May or June than October.

I swung my backpack onto one shoulder and followed Shark to the students' parking lot. I had parked my mom's little blue Chevy Malibu by the fence.

Some kids in a gym class were kicking a soccer ball back and forth on the field beside the stadium. I heard the coach's whistle and saw some other guys on the track getting in position to do sprints.

"Hey, Nate—leaving early?"

I heard the shout and spun around. Aaron. Calling from the soccer field.

I waved. And saw Candy watching us from

beside the track. She wore white gym shorts and a gray T-shirt. Her black hair flew around her face in the warm breeze. She had her hands on her waist and stared hard at us, squinting into the sun.

I spun away from her. Up ahead, Shark had his head down. He took long, loping strides. I had to run to catch up to him.

"I just want to get out of here," he muttered. He shook his head. "I'd like to get in the car and start driving and just keep going. I mean, never look back. Just keep following the highway wherever it leads."

"Whoa. What's up?" I asked. That didn't sound like Shark.

Well, yes, it did. I mean, you never knew what you were going to get with him. Some days he was up and enthusiastic and really into things. Other days . . .

"You mean the thing at the bar last night?" I asked. "The cockroaches?"

He shook his head. "That's not what I was thinking about, Nate."

I unlocked the car door and started to slide into the driver's seat. "What were you thinking about?"

He shrugged. "Whatever." He suddenly looked embarrassed.

"No. Really," I said.

He gazed at me a long time, as if deciding what to tell me. "It's my dad," he said finally, lowering his eyes. "He . . . he gets drunk every night. I think my mom . . . I think she's had it. I mean, she says she can't take it anymore. You should hear the yelling and screaming."

He kept his eyes down. His hand tapped the side of the car, beating out a fast, tense rhythm. "It's everything, Nate. I mean, my grades totally suck this term. And . . . well . . . Nikki. You know. I mean, I don't want a *relationship* or anything. But she's talking all the time about the two of us being a couple or something. I mean . . ."

His voice trailed off. I'd seen him like this before. He usually snapped out of it in a day or two.

"Maybe it's Nights," I said. "Maybe you're just wrecked, Shark. Maybe you should stay home and sleep and—"

"No way!" he said sharply. "Late at night in the bar—that's the only quiet time I get. That's the only time it's like . . . peaceful, you know?"

He rubbed his temples as if he had a headache.

I turned back. Candy was still watching us. She stood there beside the track like a statue, hands on her waist, not moving.

Was she trying to freak me out?

Shark moved to the other side of the car and pulled open the passenger door. He tossed his backpack into the back seat.

I heard voices. Ada and Jamie came hurrying across the parking lot, their shoes thudding on the asphalt.

Ada jogged toward us, shouting our names. Jamie tried to keep up with her, but her bad leg kept her several paces behind.

They didn't say a word. Just squeezed into the back seat of my little two-door car. "Where are we going?" Ada asked.

I pulled my door shut. Shark crushed a Burger King cup on the floor and tossed it out the window. I turned the ignition and the car started up. I floored the gas pedal a few times, making the engine roar.

"Jamie? Cutting class?" I said. "Aren't you afraid of messing up your grade point average?"

"I took the stupid course last year," she

said. She straightened her dark hair behind her shoulders. One of her long, silvery earrings tangled in her hair, and she struggled to pull it out. "I can't believe they're making me repeat this stuff."

Ada blew a big, pink bubblegum bubble. Shark reached back and popped it. Bubblegum splattered over her face. "Nice, Shark," she said. "Welcome to kindergarten."

I tore out of the parking lot with my tires squealing.

"Great way to sneak out of school," Jamie said.

"Who cares?" Shark replied.

Ada, Jamie, and I talked and kidded around while Shark sat in silence. He kept his eyes straight ahead and didn't seem to be listening to the conversation.

Soon we were on the River Road, which curves along the shores of the Onononka River. A forest of thick pine trees whirred past on our right. To the left, tall reeds poked up from the grassy shoreline of the river.

The road curves along the water, then climbs to high rock cliffs. The wooded clearings on top of the cliffs are a popular parking spot for Shadyside High kids looking for . . . you know . . . some privacy.

But I didn't follow the road up. Instead I hit the brakes hard, squealed to a stop, then turned into a wide, grassy clearing between clusters of tall reeds.

We climbed out of the car, pulled off our shoes, and made our way along the muddy shore to the river. The girls and I held back, but Shark stepped into the water. He tugged up the legs of his jeans and let the water wash over his ankles.

"How is it?" I called.

"Freezing cold," Shark replied. "Feels good." He took another step, and the water rolled over the bottoms of his jeans.

"Whoa!" Shark shouted. "The bottom—it drops straight down. It's totally deep here."

I waded in for a second, but the icy water made my ankles ache. I hobbled back, shaking the pain from one foot, then the other.

The two girls and I found a sunny, dry spot in the grass. We dropped down and stretched out and raised our faces to the sun.

Shark splashed along the shore for a while. Then he began picking up stones and heaving them with all his strength into the river. He tossed one after another, grunting with each throw, his face tight and intense as if he was having some kind of contest with himself.

Finally Jamie called for him to come and sit down. To my surprise, Shark obeyed. He stretched out between the two girls, pulled up a fat blade of grass, and jammed it between his lips.

"What's your problem, anyway?" Jamie asked him. She was leaning back with her hands in the grass. Her dark eyes caught the light of the sun.

Shark scratched one shoulder. "Don't really know."

"You looked so intense," Ada said. "What were you thinking about?"

He frowned. "Cockroaches."

Jamie turned to me. "That was so freaky last night," she said. "I couldn't get to sleep, Nate. I kept thinking they were in my bed."

Shark chewed on the blade of grass. He kept his eyes down.

"It's so gross," Ada murmured. "I'm so glad I stayed home last night. I mean . . . crawling on your *tongue*?"

"Stop talking about it," I said sharply. "I can't stop thinking about it either. My mouth has been itching all day."

I picked a ladybug off the knee of my jeans, dropped it into my other hand, and watched it cross my palm. "Did you see the look on Candy's face?" I asked. "When I had the cockroaches climbing out of my mouth?"

Jamie and Shark shook their heads. "Candy *is* a cockroach," Shark muttered.

"Well, she was grinning," I said. "I mean, she had this big grin on her face, like she was so enjoying it."

"You're joking," Ada murmured.

"Candy is a witch!" Jamie exclaimed. "That explains it. She cast some kind of spell on you, Nate. Then she sat back and watched."

Ada laughed.

"That's dumb," Shark said.

Jamie tossed a clump of dirt at him. It bounced against his T-shirt and crumbled to the grass. "It's not dumb at all. I've read a lot about witches. They really do exist."

"Dumb," Shark repeated.

"Then what's *your* explanation?" Jamie demanded.

Shark scratched his hair. "You know that story about the girl on a farm who fell asleep in the barn, and a spider crawled into her ear? It's an urban legend or something?"

Jamie shook her head. "What about it?"

"The spider laid eggs in the girl's ear canal, but she was asleep. She didn't know it," Shark continued. "And a few weeks later, she was sitting at dinner, and her ear started to itch. And hundreds of tiny spiders came crawling out of her ear."

"Oh, wow." Ada made a disgusted face. "Is that a true story?"

"Could be," Shark said.

Jamie sat up straight. "And you think Nate swallowed a cockroach sometime, and it laid eggs in his throat or something?"

"It's possible, right?" Shark replied. "And they all hatched last night." He frowned. "That's better than saying Candy is a witch and cast a spell on him."

"No way," Jamie murmured.

"Candy sure thought it was a riot," I said. "She was, like, really into it."

Shark got this faraway look in his eyes. "I know how to deal with Candy," he whispered.

"Excuse me?" Jamie asked. "What did you say?"

"I can handle Oink-Oink," Shark said.

"What are you going to do?" I asked.

Shark didn't answer. He climbed to his feet and started to walk rapidly to the shore.

"Where are you going?" Jamie called after him.

He turned back. "For a walk. Want to come?"

Jamie struggled to her feet and took off after Shark. Ada and I sat side by side in the grass and watched them disappear behind a clump of tall evergreen shrubs.

"The cockroach thing is totally creepy," Ada said, turning to me. "You must have been so scared, Nate." Her eyes were kinda watery, and her chin trembled.

Before I could reply, she grabbed my head with both hands and pulled my face to hers. She started kissing me, kissing me hard, moving her lips against mine.

Stunned, it took me a little while to kiss her back.

Ada had never been into me in any way. But here we were, holding each other, pressing against each other in the warm grass, and lip-locked so hard I could barely breathe.

I wrapped my arms around her waist as I kissed her. I felt her mouth open. Our kiss lasted for another minute or two. Then she suddenly pulled away. Her face was red, like she was embarrassed.

I wanted to act casual about it. You know, be cool. But I didn't really know how to do that. I just stared at her wide-eyed, breathing hard, until she laughed.

Was she laughing at me? Or laughing because she liked me? *Did* she like me?

I didn't have time to think about it because I saw Shark and Jamie returning from their walk. I jumped to my feet and brushed off my jeans with both hands. And pretended that scene with Ada had never happened.

"Let's go," Shark said.

I grabbed Ada's hands and tugged her to her feet. Her face was still red, and she had a strange smile frozen there.

We walked to the car, put on our shoes, and climbed back in—Shark and me in front, the girls in back.

I fumbled in my jeans pocket and found

the key. The car started right up. "Hey, this beats seventh-period government," Shark said.

"We should do this *every* afternoon," I said.

"You couldn't do that, Nate. You're such a *good* boy," Ada said.

Now she was teasing me. What was up with her?

I shifted into reverse and lowered my foot on the gas pedal. I felt a jolt.

The car jerked forward.

"Whoa!" I let out a cry of surprise.

My right hand tightened on the gearshift at my side. I jammed it forward, then back into reverse.

The engine roared. The car bumped over the grass, picking up speed, shooting to the water.

"It won't back up!" I screamed.

I jammed my foot down on the brake.

I waited for the car to stop. No. The car picked up speed.

I slammed my foot down on the brake again. Again.

I froze in panic as I realized the car wasn't stopping.

We all screamed as it roared over the side of the shore.

I gripped the steering wheel with both hands as the car flew through the air, engine roaring.

Our screams stopped as we soared up, then crashed into the water, splashing up tall waves all around us.

The car rocked on the surface for a few moments.

"Open the doors!" Ada shrieked. "Open them! Get out! Get out! Hurry!"

I couldn't move. I felt dazed. Dizzy.

This couldn't be happening!

We were sinking, sinking fast to the bottom of the river.

"We're going to drown!" Ada wailed. "We're all going to drown!"

16

Dark green water rose halfway up the car windows. The car rocked hard, tilting to one side then the other as it sank to the bottom.

I grabbed my door handle and jerked it hard. I shoved my shoulder into the door.

The door wouldn't budge.

I jammed my shoulder into the door again.

No. It wouldn't move.

My heart thudded in my chest. I heard Jamie and Ada screaming in the back seat.

Ada shoved the back of my seat. "Open the door, Nate! Open the door!" She screamed the words over and over.

I turned to Shark. He was staring straight ahead, eyes wide. Watching the dark water rise up over the windshield. His hand pressed against the dashboard. His mouth hung open in horror.

"Shark! Shark! Your door!" I choked out.

I grabbed him by the shoulder and shook him. "Your door! Your door!"

It took a few seconds for him to come to life. He swung away from me and started to struggle with the handle.

"It's leaking in! Hurry! It's leaking in!" Ada shrieked, banging the back of my seat with her fists.

I pulled the door handle again and leaned into the door with all my strength.

"Oh!" I uttered a cry as the car hit the river bottom. A hard jolt sent me flying off the seat. Then the car floated up again.

Shark and I both pushed our weight against the doors. His door swung open, and water rushed in with a loud *whoosh*. I saw him push himself into the rushing water.

"Hurry! Hurry!" Ada screamed from behind me.

And then my door swung open. I didn't shut my mouth in time, and water roared into my throat.

Choking, sputtering, I kicked hard. Kicked

myself free of the car and went floating into the river.

The icy water froze me in shock. I couldn't move my arms and legs.

How long did it take? I don't know. When my body finally adjusted to the cold, I spun back to the car. Squinting through the murky water, I could see Ada's arms flailing out of the open car door.

Her hair floated straight up above her face. Her arms waved frantically in the water. Her eyes were wide with terror.

It took me a little while to realize she was stuck. Stuck in the back seat.

My chest began to ache. I needed fresh air. But I lowered myself in the water. I dropped to the side of the car.

A cluster of thick, greasy weeds swept around my face. I tugged them off, tried to toss them aside.

Bending low, I fumbled for the lever on the back of the passenger seat. I couldn't see in the darkness of the water. It took me a long while to find it.

Ada grabbed me by the hair. She pulled hard. Panic swept over me. If I didn't find the lever, she'd drown. We'd *both* drown.

Finally I clicked the lever. The force of Ada's weight sent the seat back rolling forward.

I floated up and grabbed her hands. She squeezed my hands so tightly her nails dug deep into my skin. Ignoring the pain, I pulled her out of the car.

A few seconds later, our heads rose over the surface. We both choked and gasped and sucked in air noisily.

I realized I was still grasping Ada's hands. She pulled away from me and started to splash to the shore.

My chest throbbing, I spun around in the water. Squinting into the fading sunlight, I saw Shark bobbing on the surface.

He raised a hand over his head and waved to me. Then he came swimming toward me.

I crawled onto the shore and lay facedown in the wet grass. I sucked in breath after breath. I couldn't seem to catch up.

My whole body shivered. My clothes held the iciness of the water. My hair was matted wetly over my face.

Using my last remaining strength, I pulled myself to my feet. I saw Ada and Shark huddled against the wide trunk of a tree.

"J–Jamie?" I stammered. I grabbed the tree trunk to hold myself up.

I saw the frightened expressions on Ada and Shark. With great effort, Shark pulled himself to his knees and stared out to the water.

"Jamie?"

And then all three of us began to shout her name.

"Jamie! Jamie! Jamie?"

The river rolled rapidly past us. I saw tangles of weeds swimming like eels in the current.

No sign of her. No sign.

My breath caught in my throat. My legs gave way and I fell to the muddy ground.

"Jamie? Where are you?"

"Jamie?"

No.

No. No.

Ada and Shark were still screaming her name. I grabbed Shark by the shoulder. My voice came out in a choked whisper: "Why isn't she coming up? *Why?*"

17

Gripped with horror, I gazed out at the rippling water. My stomach lurched. I couldn't stop shivering.

And I couldn't stop shouting Jamie's name.

No sign of her. I couldn't even see the car. Just the dark water, flowing by so softly, steadily, as if nothing had happened.

Gasping for breath, I grabbed Shark by the arm. "We have to g-get her," I choked out.

Shark's eyes were wide and his mouth hung open. He kept shaking his head. "Too late," he whispered. "It's been too long, Nate."

Ada buried her face in her hands. Her shoulders heaved up and down. Loud sobs escaped her throat.

"Too late . . . ," Shark repeated, as if in a daze.

"Shark—we have to try!" I cried, jerking his arm hard, trying to snap him out of it. "Shark—"

I didn't wait for him. I took off running into the water. When it rose over my knees, I did a surface dive.

The river bottom dropped away sharply, and I pulled myself down. It took a few seconds to find the car. It stood still, anchored on the muddy river bottom, both doors open.

Jamie—where are you? Why didn't you get out?

Is it really too late?

Yes. I knew it had been nearly five minutes.

Too late . . . too late to be alive.

I pictured Jamie . . . her warm smile . . . would I never see it again?

I felt something move in the water. Startled, I glanced back—and saw Shark swimming hard, close behind me.

I grabbed the open car door and swung myself down. I pushed away a clump of weeds and peered through the murky water into the car.

Jamie stared out at me, her dark brown eyes

open wide. Glassy. Lifeless. Her expression a blank.

My heart skipped a beat. I could feel all my muscles tighten.

I'd never seen a dead person before.

I'd never seen a drowned person before.

A drowned friend . . .

I must have blacked out for a moment. The next thing I knew, Shark had shoved me out of the way. Kicking hard, he lowered himself into the car.

He grabbed Jamie's hands and pulled.

Her body caught on the back of the seat. Her eyes stared at me, empty and wide, not blinking. Her mouth was shut tight, her jaw clenched.

My chest started to ache. I needed to breathe. But I lowered myself beside Shark and took Jamie's hands. They felt limp and lifeless.

Shark gripped her under the shoulders. I pulled her by the hands. She caught against the seat one more time, then slid loose.

Her dark hair floated around her head as we carried her to the surface. We both rose over the water, choking and gasping for air.

Jamie wasn't breathing. I could see that.

Her eyes shut. Her mouth dropped open. Murky river water poured out of her mouth.

We dragged her onto shore. Ada helped us set her down. Ada's cheeks were red and swollen. She had tears running down her face. Dead leaves were caught in her hair.

"I know CPR," Ada said in a trembling voice. "Put her on her back."

Shark and I turned her over. She felt like a heavy sack. I knew she wasn't breathing.

"Too late . . . ," Shark murmured. "It's too late."

But Ada went to work.

She knelt beside Jamie, clamped two fingers over Jamie's nose, and began blowing into her mouth. One . . . two . . . one . . . two . . . blowing into Jamie's mouth in a steady rhythm.

Then she climbed onto Jamie's waist and began pumping her chest with both hands. Pushing rapidly on her chest, again and again.

More water spewed from Jamie's open mouth.

"Too late," Shark repeated, shaking his head. "It's been over five minutes. She . . . she . . ."

Jamie uttered a groan.

Her whole body kicked. She groaned again. She opened her eyes. And vomited loudly onto the ground.

Choking, vomiting up puddles of green glop, she blinked her eyes, gaping at us as if she didn't recognize us.

"She's ALIVE!" I shouted. My heart was leaping around in my chest. I wanted to jump up and down for joy. "She's ALIVE!"

Shark and I slapped each other high-fives.

Ada wiped Jamie's mouth with the sleeve of her soaked T-shirt. "Are you okay? Are you really okay?" Tears streamed down Ada's face.

We pulled Jamie up to a sitting position and leaned her against the tree trunk. She blinked at us, shaking her head, shivering. She brushed her hair off her forehead.

"Hi," she said finally.

"Jamie? You're okay?" I asked, squatting beside her, grabbing her hand. It felt alive now. Her fingers squeezed back.

"Yeah, I guess," she said. She gazed around. Her eyes stopped on me. "What happened?"

"My car plunged into the water," I said. "Don't you remember?"

She thought about it for a long moment, then shook her head.

"You were trapped under there for a long time," Ada said, leaning on my shoulders. "We thought . . . we thought . . ."

Jamie let out a long, loud burp. "I guess I'm all right. I mean, I feel kinda weird. But I'm okay."

"Man, you were under so long!" Shark exclaimed. "How did you hold your breath so long?"

Jamie crinkled up her face, thinking hard. "I guess all that time on the swim team? I must have really built up my lung power."

I shivered. "We've got to get home. Get dry clothes."

"How? We're stuck out here," Ada said.

I pulled my cell phone out of my pocket. It was soaked, but would it work?

I shook it. Water came spraying off. I tried to call home.

No. The phone was dead.

I turned and saw Shark trying his phone.

Yes! He was speaking to his dad.

I breathed a sigh of relief. After all the horror of the afternoon, I didn't think we could walk ten miles home.

"Dad'll be here in a few minutes," Shark said, clicking his phone shut.

Leaning on the tree trunk, Jamie climbed unsteadily to her feet. She took a few shaky steps. "I . . . I'm okay," she told us.

She turned to me. "Why'd you drive into the river? I mean, what happened to your car, anyway?"

Once again I remembered shifting the car into reverse. Remembered stomping down hard on the brake.

The car ignored me.

The car shot forward on its own.

I frowned at Jamie. I suddenly had all kinds of crazy thoughts in my head. Crazy, weird thoughts. . . .

"Maybe you're right about the witch's spell," I murmured. "Maybe you're totally right, Jamie. Maybe Candy *is* a witch."

18

Had Candy put a curse on me? Was she casting spells? Because of the pig photo? Because she thought I was responsible for it?

The cockroaches . . . the car flying into the river . .

It didn't take much to put two and two together—and realize something totally unnatural was going down.

But was it possible? Was I really starting to believe that Candy somehow had evil powers? That Candy was doing these things to me?

How crazy is that?

About a week later, the day I got the car back . . . that's when we decided we had to investigate. We had to do everything we could to find out the truth.

At about two in the morning on a drizzly

Thursday night, four of us—all guys—were sitting in the back booth at Nights. Shark and I were there. And Lewis. And then Galen came in, shaking off rainwater.

Shark seemed thoughtful tonight, and quiet. He sipped from his beer bottle and kept his gaze on the front of the bar.

"I got my car back," I said.

"Whoa. Was it totally waterlogged?" Galen asked.

I shook my head. "They got it all dried out. My mom has a really awesome mechanic at a garage in the Old Village. Would you believe it runs like new?"

They stared at me. "Dude, what was wrong with it?" Shark asked. "I mean, was the transmission shot or something? Why wouldn't it go in reverse?"

I shrugged. "Beats me. The mechanic couldn't find anything wrong."

"But the brakes . . ." Shark said. "You pumped them and pumped them, remember? And we went flying into the river . . . ?"

"The brakes work fine now," I said. "Once the car dried out, they worked fine. No problem."

"But, Nate—," Shark started.

"It's a total mystery," I said. "I'm totally creeped out."

I shuddered, thinking about Jamie.

She almost drowned.

How could there be nothing wrong with the car?

She almost drowned.

"The car just took off on its own," Shark said in a whisper. "I don't get it."

That's when Lewis started talking about ghosts. About how here we were, sitting on the very spot where the Fear Mansion had stood. And maybe a lot of ghosts were disturbed when they tore down the old mansion.

Galen laughed and said Lewis had seen too many horror flicks. But Shark told Lewis to keep talking.

"Jamie has this thing about ghosts," Lewis said. "You know. Ever since her cousin Cindy died, Jamie's been trying to reach her."

He took a long drink from his can of Coke. "One night we went to the Fear Mansion after it had been torn down. We stayed out all night, trying to contact a ghost."

He sighed. "I thought it was a big joke. I didn't believe in ghosts . . ."

"But you do now?" I interrupted.

Lewis nodded. "Yeah. We got a woman's voice on tape. Very faint. But we could hear her. It was real. She was a real ghost. We taped her right here where the bar was built. Right on this spot." He tapped the table.

I stared at him. "What happened to the tape?"

"Yeah. Can you play it for us?" Galen asked.

Lewis shook his head. "It disappeared. After that night Jamie and I fell in . . . after our accident . . . we couldn't find it."

I frowned at Lewis. "And you think a ghost made the cockroaches pour out of my mouth? And made my car go out of control?"

"Maybe a ghost," Lewis said. "Maybe it's some kind of Fear Street curse. Or evil spell. Or maybe it's Candy getting back at you, Nate. Maybe she found a spell book or something that night in the hidden room. It's possible."

The four of us fell silent.

I didn't know what to believe. What Lewis was saying sounded totally wacko to me. I didn't want to believe in any of that. I didn't want to believe Candy could cast spells. And I didn't want to believe that old Fear Street ghosts were on the loose.

But how *do* you explain what had happened?

I stared at Shark. *We almost* died *in my car,* I thought. And the mechanic couldn't find anything wrong with it.

"We can't just sit here and wait for something else to happen," I said. "We've got to find out who or what is doing this to us."

Could we solve the mystery before the horror started again?

Actually, no.

PART FOUR

19

On Monday afternoon I went into the computer lab at school to Google some stuff I needed for a term paper. Shadyside High has a good computer lab with two long rows of cubicles. About twenty in all. Each cubicle has a desktop networked to a fast DSL line.

As I walked in I saw that the lab was pretty empty. Two ninth-grade guys huddled in the first cubicle playing Free Cell. At the end of the back row I saw Jamie typing away, concentrating hard on something.

Shark and Ada sat on high stools in a cubicle near the wall. Shark had headphones on. He was tapping his fingers in a fast rhythm on the tabletop. They both stared into the glare of the monitor.

"What's up?" I asked Ada.

She shrugged. "Not much. I'm helping Shark find stuff he needs for his project."

"Project?" I turned to the screen. Shark appeared to be downloading songs from iTunes.

I reached over and tugged off Shark's headphones. "What's up with this?" I asked.

"Hey, Nate. How's it going? I'm downloading some jazz stuff. Mr. Hernandez said I could do my term paper on fusion jazz. You know. I'm kinda into that. So I'm making a mix to go with my term paper."

"Cool," I said. I examined the headphones. "Nice."

He took them back from me. "Yeah, I brought them from home. They're Bose. They were a birthday present. They're amazing."

Ada tugged at a silvery necklace that fell over her dark blue top. "Check this out, Nate. Cool, isn't it? It's real silver."

"Very cool," I said. "Was it your mom's?"

"No way. I found it that night. You know. At the Fear Mansion. My mom says it's a really old antique. I've had it hidden in the back of a drawer for a year. But, hey, why not wear it?"

"You should sell it," Shark said.

"No way. I'm keeping it. Is that all you think of? Just money?"

"Yeah," Shark said.

Ada gave him a shove that almost knocked him off his stool.

I heard the door to the computer lab close. I turned and saw Candy stride into the room. She carried her backpack at her side. She glanced around the room, studied the two boys playing Free Cell for a moment, then saw us.

I thought maybe she'd avoid us and go the other way. But a smile crossed her face, and she came hurrying over.

She wore very tight, low-riding jeans and a sleeveless pink midriff top that left about two inches of skin showing. She had a nice tan. Her parents had taken her to Paradise Island over Columbus Day weekend.

I saw she had that jeweled pendant on a chain around her neck. I think she never took it off.

Shark pulled on his headphones and turned to the computer. Ada and I looked away too. We thought maybe she'd take the hint.

But Candy seemed determined to talk to

us. She stood there staring at Shark until he was forced to turn around. "What's up?" he asked her, staring at her bare stomach.

She hesitated. Her cheeks turned pink. She fingered the glittering pendant. "This isn't easy for me," she said finally. "But . . . maybe we all should make up." She turned to me.

Shark just stared at her, as if he didn't understand the words. Ada and I exchanged glances.

The pink circles on Candy's cheeks darkened to red. "I mean, we should start over. I don't like having enemies, you know. We've known each other since fifth grade, right?"

Shark didn't respond at all.

Candy let out a sigh. "Nate, help me out here. I'm trying to be, like, nice. You know."

"That's great," I said without any enthusiasm. I didn't know what to say.

She shifted her backpack to her other hand. "Well, anyway, guys, my parents are going away this weekend. I'm inviting a bunch of kids Saturday night to come over and party. I thought maybe you three . . ." Her voice trailed off. She kept her eyes on me.

Shark grinned at her. "Oh, wow, I'm busy

Saturday night. I have to stay home and take out the trash."

Ada burst out laughing.

It was mean, but I couldn't help it—I laughed too.

Candy's expression didn't change. She just kept staring at me. One hand held on to the backpack strap. The other hand was wrapped around the pendant.

"I can't make it either," I said.

"Why not?" Candy asked.

I shrugged. "I don't know. Just can't."

Her eyes burned into mine. Her cheeks turned dark red.

"Okay," she said softly. She turned and walked quickly out of the computer lab. She didn't look back.

The door closed behind her.

Shark let out a giggle. Ada slapped him on the shoulder. "That was totally nasty," she said. "Why did you do that?"

Shark's grin faded. "She deserves it." He started to turn back to the monitor.

But I made a grab for the headphones. "Let me try them," I said.

Shark scooted out of the way. He showed

me the volume control. "Here. Double-click this song. Crank it up," he said.

I slid the headphones over my ears and adjusted them. I clicked on the song and started to listen. After a few seconds, I was nodding my head in time to the music. The sound was amazing. I flashed Shark a thumbs-up.

I let out a gasp when I felt something wet on the sides of my head. At first I didn't realize what it was. Sweat? Something on the headphones?

I glanced down and saw two splashes of red on the floor.

"Hey!" I jerked off the headphones. And I screamed as bright red blood spurted—spurted straight out from both of my ears.

It felt so strange. Like my ears were open faucets. Two powerful streams of blood came spraying out. Streaming like a fountain . . . spraying the cubicle walls . . . staining the floor all around me. The sound of it roared in my ears.

This isn't happening! I told myself. *This is impossible.*

My mouth wide in shock and horror, I pressed my hands against my ears. The roaring stopped. But the blood streamed over my hands, flowed down my arms, and on to the shoulders of my white T-shirt.

I felt weak. Dizzy. I dropped my hands, and the blood spurted straight out again, twin fountains.

"Hey!" Shark and Ada both cried out as a stream of blood splashed over them. They ducked and dodged out of the way.

The blood splashed against the walls.

My stomach lurched. The roaring in my ears was deafening. I saw Shark splattered with blood, staring in disbelief, unable to move or cry out.

And then I finally found my voice and started to scream. High, shrill cries of pain and terror.

"Help me! *Please*—HELP ME!"

20

Ada grabbed my arm. Shark took the other arm. Blood streamed from my ears onto the cubicle walls, puddling on the floor at our feet. They both grabbed me and led me out of the computer lab.

I pressed my hands against my ears, frantically trying to stop the flow. I heard kids screaming and crying out. But they were just a blur to me.

The blood washed over my face, my shirt. But I concentrated on walking, my legs suddenly rubbery and weak. Walking past the startled, horrified kids, down the next hall, to Miss Hanley's office.

We burst into the small, narrow office. Miss Hanley was bending over a kid on the couch, taking his temperature. She dropped the thermometer when she saw me, saw the streams of blood, and heard my weak screams.

"Quick—over here," she said, guiding us into the back room. Miss Hanley lowered me onto a cot. She stuffed big wads of cotton into my ears.

"What happened? How did this happen?" She couldn't hide the fear from her voice.

I lay on the cot pressing the cotton wads to my ears, so weak, dizzy from losing so much blood.

"We—we don't know," I choked out.

"Nate just started to bleed," Shark said, shaking his head.

I closed my eyes. I felt faint. As if I were fading . . . fading into sleep.

"We need to get an ambulance," Miss Hanley said in a trembling voice. "I . . . I don't understand this."

She reached for the phone on her desk.

I opened my eyes. "Hey—," I called out. "Hey—I think it stopped."

Miss Hanson dropped the phone and hurried back to me. She moved my hands away from the cotton wads and carefully removed them.

In the wall mirror, I could see that my ears were stained red. I could see dark, lumpy clots stuck to my earlobes. But the blood wasn't pouring out anymore.

I let out a long sigh of relief.

Shark sighed too and dropped onto the empty cot across from me.

"Yes, it seems to have stopped," Miss Hanley said. She bent to examine my ears. "I . . . I've never seen anything like this."

I groaned and started to sit up, but Miss Hanley gently pushed me back down. "Don't stand up. You've lost a lot of blood. You may need to replenish it."

"You—you mean—transfusions?" My voice was weak, just a whisper.

"I'm calling your mother," Miss Hanley said. "Then an ambulance. You need to be checked out by a doctor."

I sank back on the cot and shut my eyes. I still felt shaky. My heart was pounding like crazy.

I was covered in blood. The blood had caked onto my shirt and jeans. It smelled sour, kind of metallic.

"You and Ada had better go home and

change," the nurse told Shark. "Good work bringing Nate in here."

Shark climbed to his feet. He and Ada started to the door, stepping over the trail of blood from the hall.

Candy walked into the doorway, her face red and tight with worry. "Is Nate okay? Is he going to be okay?"

"He's doing better," Miss Hanley said. "That's all I can say."

Candy pushed past Shark up to my cot. "You look so pale," she said. She narrowed her eyes and stared at the clotted blood on my ears. "How do you feel?"

I mumbled a reply.

Shark stepped up to Candy. "How did you know Nate was in here?" he asked. "How did you know Nate was in trouble?"

A strange smile spread over Candy's face. "I saw him in the hall," she said. "What did you think?"

21

Two nights later I sat in the back booth at Nights. I still felt shaky, a little weak. And mainly, tense. I kept waiting for something else to happen. Wondering what would happen to me next.

I hadn't slept. I had no appetite. I couldn't concentrate on anything. I only felt comfortable late at night with my friends at Nights.

I didn't want to believe that Candy was doing these things to me. I didn't want to believe that she somehow had found the powers to hurt me.

Yes, she blamed me for the hog picture. And maybe she knew I was the one who smashed her car window. But was that reason enough to try to kill me?

No way. I didn't want to believe it was Candy.

But *what else* could I believe?

I took a long sip of beer. I wanted to get trashed tonight. Maybe it would calm me down. Maybe for just a few minutes I could stop being afraid of every sound, every movement around me. Afraid of my own body.

Jamie and Lewis sat at a booth near the back, and I saw Candy at a back table talking with two girls from Waynesbridge. She had her back to me, so she couldn't give me her usual evil eye.

I looked up and saw Galen walk in. He had a blue Cubs cap pulled sideways over his coppery hair. He wore baggy jeans under a faded red and gray Beastie Boys T-shirt.

"Hey, guys. Whassup?" he shouted. Just about everyone in the bar turned to look at him. "I've got it!" he called. "Nate—dude! I know why these things are happening to you! I mean, it's unbelievable. You're not going to *believe* what I found out."

Whoa.

What did Galen find out? My heart started to pound like crazy.

Galen started past the bar, but Ryland raised a hand. He dropped the towel he was using to wipe beer glasses. "Hey, Galen—aren't you forgetting something?"

Galen stared at Ryland for a moment. "Oh. Yeah."

He backed up to the brass plaque of Simon and Angelica Fear on the wall. "Nate, wait till you hear what I found," he shouted. "We're going to need all the good luck we can get!"

He lowered his head to the plaque and kissed it, just above Angelica Fear's forehead. It was a very long kiss.

I leaned forward over the table and watched as Galen kept his lips pressed to the plaque. Why was he taking so long?

Was he trying to be funny, showing off what a great kisser he was?

No. It didn't take long to see that it was no joke.

Galen started to squirm. He pulled back. But his lips . . .

. . . His lips stayed stuck to the plaque.

He let out a muffled shout. It took me a while to realize he was calling for help.

Galen had both hands pressed against the

wall and was pushing back. But his mouth didn't move off the plaque.

His face turned bright red. His Cubs cap fell off and dropped to the floor.

His cries grew louder. He twisted his head up and down and from side to side. He pushed off the wall with both hands.

It grew really quiet in the bar. Shark and I jumped to our feet. We went running to the front.

Ryland hurried out from behind the bar. He had his hand on Galen's shoulder. "Calm, calm," he kept repeating.

Sweat poured down Galen's face. He shouted something, but I couldn't understand him. He tugged back again—and cried out in pain. I could see that his lips were stuck tight to the plaque.

"I don't get it," Ryland said, scratching his spiky hair. "This is totally weird. This can't be happening."

My heart was pounding. I wanted to help—but *how*?

"Do you have any grease or anything?" Shark asked.

Ryland stared back at him.

Galen let out another shrill cry of pain. He kept trying to tell us something. But his mouth was stuck tight.

Ryland turned to the bar. "I'm going to call the fire department," he said. "Maybe they can deal with this. I—"

"No—wait!" Shark said. He grabbed Ryland by the shoulder. "If you call them, we'll all be busted. They'll report us. Our parents will find out we've been sneaking out."

Galen's cries were weaker now. His face had gone pale. His hair glistened with sweat.

"Try some butter," I said, finally finding my voice. "You've got butter, right?"

Ryland hesitated. Then he moved to a small refrigerator under the bar. He bent down and started fumbling around inside it.

Galen whimpered in pain. I turned to him. "We'll get you off that thing," I said. "Just stay calm, okay? Don't move. Just wait."

Galen mumbled a reply, but again I couldn't understand.

"Weird," Ryland was muttering. "Too weird." He brought over a half stick of butter.

Shark took it from him and started to smear it on the plaque. Galen let out a scream when the stick of butter bumped his lips.

Shark carefully, gently applied the butter, smearing it over the brass. Lowering it to Galen's mouth. Spreading it all around Galen's lips.

"If this doesn't work, I'm dialing 911," Ryland said. He shook his head. "I don't get this. I just don't."

The butter had softened and oozed over Shark's fingers. He took a step back. "Nate, try to move Galen's head," he instructed me. "Very gently. Give it a try."

My hands started shaking as I raised them. I placed them carefully on the sides of Galen's head. Then slowly . . . carefully . . . I tried to slide his mouth over the buttery surface.

But no. No . . .

His mouth wouldn't move.

Galen uttered a sharp cry of pain.

I gasped and jerked my hands away. I staggered back, startled by his cry.

And to my surprise, Galen staggered back with me.

We both toppled backward into the bar.

Yes!

He was free!

Galen was free. The butter had worked.

I started to open my mouth in a cheer of victory.

But then I raised my eyes to the wall. To the plaque . . .

And I saw . . .

I saw a piece of Galen's tongue   and both of his lips—*still stuck to the plaque.*

22

Ryland got Galen to the emergency room at Shadyside General. The rest of us all scurried home. Galen was definitely busted. Now his parents would know about him sneaking out to Nights. But we knew he wouldn't rat out the rest of us.

Of course, all that didn't matter much to Galen. The poor guy was totally messed up. He needed surgery and spent a couple of weeks in the hospital.

I tried calling him there. A woman picked up the phone. Maybe it was a nurse or maybe it was his mom. She said Galen had a lot of stitches and couldn't talk very well.

I kept picturing that red chunk of tongue stuck to the brass plaque like a piece of raw hamburger. And the two thin, cut lips. And each time I thought about it I felt sick, like I was going to hurl my guts out.

I had to force that picture from my mind. But then I kept thinking about what Galen had said when he walked into the bar.

He said he'd found out why things were happening to me. He said he knew the truth.

My mind kept spinning with ideas. What had Galen found out?

Did someone try to keep him from telling?

If only he could talk. I had to know what he'd learned. I had to hear it before . . . before something else happened to me.

A couple of weeks after Galen had been hospitalized, Shark and I were walking to my house. A car horn made me jump.

We turned to see Jamie pull up in her blue Corolla. Lewis sat beside her. They both called out, "Hi!"

"Hey, what's up?" I called.

"Galen is home," Jamie said. "He got home last night. His mom said he can have visitors."

"Have you seen him?" I asked.

"Yeah. Lewis and I just came from there," Jamie replied.

"How is he?" I asked.

She shrugged. "He's all stitched up. But he can talk pretty well. He's going to need plastic surgery."

A car honked behind Jamie. She gave us a wave and drove on.

"Let's go see him," Shark said.

We turned and walked to Galen's house. He lives in a tiny white brick house about two blocks from Fear Street Acres.

He has three sisters. He says the house is so small that he's always bumping into one of them. He says he comes to Nights for the peace and quiet.

Galen's mother was just leaving when Shark and I walked up the drive. She opened the front door for us and said Galen would be really glad to see us.

Two of his sisters were in the living room playing a Super Mario game on the TV. We found Galen in his tiny bedroom in the back of the house. He sat up in bed when he saw us.

"Hey, whassup?" He put down the copy of *Sports Illustrated* he'd been reading. He kinda lisped. He said "whatthup" instead of "whassup."

Shark and I tried to find a place to sit in

the little room. It was the size of a closet. No kidding. It probably *was* a closet.

"How's it going, Galen?" Shark asked.

I couldn't stop staring at his mouth. It was totally swollen and covered with black stitches. He had little pieces of black thread poking out of his skin.

"Not bad," he said. "I won't be kissing any girls for a while." He lisped all the s's.

Shark and I both laughed. You know. Awkward, forced laughter.

But Galen didn't laugh. He suddenly got real serious. "I . . . found out something. Something totally weird. But . . . I know what's going on. It's Candy. It's all Candy."

"Huh?" I stared at Galen. "Excuse me? Are you sure?"

Galen nodded. "Candy did this to me to keep me from talking. I know it. I tried to warn you about her, Nate, that night at the bar."

I pulled the little wooden chair from Galen's desk closer. Shark sat on the edge of the bed. He kept rolling up the copy of *Sports Illustrated* and then unrolling it.

"*Candy* made your mouth stick to the plaque?" Shark asked.

Galen nodded. "I found out the truth," he said. He cringed. I think it was painful to talk with those swollen lips. "And I know it's for real, man. All the weird things that have been going down . . . Candy did them all."

I rolled my eyes. "Galen, how many painkillers did they give you at the hospital?"

Again, he didn't laugh. "It's true. Listen to me." He climbed off the bed and started shuffling through some papers on his desk.

"I found this Web site," he said. "It's about legends and stories from the early days of Shadyside."

Galen studied one of the pages. "It's about Fear Street. All about how terrifying things happened there. And about the Fear family and how weird and evil they were."

He handed me a sheet of paper. It had a black-and-white drawing of a young woman on it.

"Check it out. Know who that is?" Galen tapped his finger on the woman's face. "Angelica Fear," he said. "She was some kinda witch, remember? We learned about her ages ago."

Shark grabbed the drawing from me and studied it. "Yeah. It's Angelica Fear. So what?"

"Check out what she's wearing," Galen said. He cringed again and raised a hand to his swollen mouth.

Shark and I both gazed at the drawing. I recognized it before Shark. "Candy's pendant!" I exclaimed.

Shark squinted at it. "Yeah. It's that same pendant Candy wears all the time. Angelica Fear is wearing it."

"The Web site has a whole page about it," Galen said. He shoved more pages into my hands. "Check it out, man. It's called an amulet. It's totally evil. The amulet has evil powers. It can be used to cast spells on people and stuff like that."

Shark and I gazed at the drawing.

"The article says it's silver with sapphire jewels on it. And look at the words on the back of the amulet," Galen said. "*Dominatio per malum*. It's Latin. My mom told me what it means. *Power through evil*."

My mind was whirring. I remembered Candy sitting in Nights with her hand wrapped around that pendant. And I remembered that big, evil grin on her face.

"Get it?" Galen demanded. "Candy has

Angelica Fear's amulet. And she's using it against us."

"The cockroaches . . ." Shark muttered, staring down at the drawing of the amulet. "The blood from your ears . . ."

"My car!" I said. "Shark—that's why my car went flying into the river."

Shark leapt to his feet. "She . . . she really did try to *kill* us!"

A chill ran down my back.

I didn't want to believe it. But here was the proof.

Candy was evil. Candy wanted to kill me.

I scanned the pages from the Web site. It was all there. Angelica Fear had used the power of the amulet to destroy her enemies . . . destroy them in ugly, painful ways.

I turned to Shark, the papers trembling in my hand. "Shark, what are we going to do?" I asked in a whisper.

Shark's eyes narrowed. "We're going to get that amulet," he said softly.

"Candy said her parents were going away," Shark said. "Remember? She was inviting kids to come over and party?"

"But no one wanted to party with her," I told Nikki. "Shark and I went by her house around nine, and there was no one there. We saw her through the window, sitting in her living room by herself."

It was a little after three in the morning, and we were at Nights. Nikki, Shark, Lewis, and I huddled at the back booth sipping beers, making a plan.

"So why didn't you go see her?" Lewis asked. "You had your perfect chance."

"No way," Shark said, spinning his beer bottle between his hands. "We have to take her by surprise."

"Shark's right," I said. "We can't just ask her for the amulet and expect she'll give it to us."

"She'll turn us into frogs or something," Shark said. He meant it as a joke, but it didn't seem too funny.

Nikki suddenly looked frightened. "Shut up! You're just going to break into her house and steal the amulet?"

"That's the plan," Shark said.

"Maybe we can do it without even waking her up," I said. I felt a sudden chill of fear. "I mean, she's dangerous. No joke. She's evil."

Lewis rolled his eyes. "I think you're crazy."

Shark tilted his head and gazed at him. "Why?"

"I think you should call the police," Lewis said. "Explain to them what Candy has been doing."

Nikki, Shark, and I laughed.

"For sure," I said. "That's perfect. Officer, a girl in our class is a witch, and she's been casting horrible spells on me. Could you arrest her and take away the evil pendant she's been using?"

Lewis let out a long sigh. "Okay, okay. You're right. That wouldn't work. But count me out. This whole plan . . . it's too dangerous. Totally. After my accident last year . . . well . . . I don't want anything to do with magic pendants or the Fear family."

"The *amulet* is too dangerous," I said. "You know me, Lewis. I usually try to talk Shark out of these crazy schemes. But this time he's right. Candy . . . she almost drowned us. You weren't there, Lewis. Jamie was barely breathing. It was the most terrifying day of my life."

"And no one will believe us about the amulet," Shark said. "We just have to do it ourselves. We have to take it away from her and hide it somewhere it will never be found."

"Well, I'm outta here," Lewis said, climbing up. "Good luck, guys. I really mean it."

We watched him walk out of the bar. He kissed the plaque on the wall on his way out. For extra luck, I guessed.

The three of us fell silent. I glanced at the Budweiser clock behind the bar. Nearly three-thirty. Ryland sat hunched on his tall stool, his back against the wall, half asleep.

I suddenly wanted to be home too. I didn't want to be breaking into Candy's house and stealing that evil amulet.

I didn't even *believe* in evil amulets!

Finally Shark turned to Nikki. He placed his hand over hers. "Are you coming with us?"

She hesitated. "I guess," she replied finally. "But I'm really frightened."

"Let's go do it," Shark said.

24

We said good night to Ryland and walked to Shark's car. It was a cold, damp night. No stars or moon in the sky. The wind kept gusting, and I felt light raindrops on my face as we walked.

I was shivering as I climbed into the back seat of the green Saturn. Shivering from the cold? From my fear?

I wasn't sure.

Nikki climbed into the front seat. Shark turned the heater up high as soon as he started the engine.

Of course there were no other cars on the street. By ten o'clock, all of Shadyside is closed up. They don't even have a midnight show at the Cineplex at the mall.

Shark drove slowly, his eyes straight ahead.

None of us said a word. I knew we were all thinking about what we were about to do.

Could we take Candy by surprise?

If we didn't, she might use the amulet on us.

I pictured Galen's swollen mouth, the lips stitched up with black thread. I pictured the bright red blood shooting from my ears, spraying the walls, the floor—and everyone.

I swallowed.

I hugged myself to stop the shivers.

Angelica Fear had used that amulet. A hundred years ago, she had used that same amulet to *kill* people.

And now Candy had it.

And she *hated* me.

Shark cut the headlights about half a block from Candy's house. The car slid silently to the curb and stopped at the driveway.

I peered up at the house through the car window. Completely dark.

I saw Candy's BMW parked in the drive at the side.

We climbed out of the car, closing the doors silently and quickly so the roof light would go out. A strong gust of cold greeted us as if trying to push us away.

The three of us huddled together at the bottom of the drive, gazing up at the dark house. Trees shook and rattled in the wind. The rain began to patter down harder.

Nikki leaned against Shark. She had her arm tucked around his. Her hair blew behind her in the gusting wind. I saw that she was shivering, too.

She turned to Shark. "Are we really doing this?"

Shark pulled away from her and took a few steps up the asphalt drive. He wiped rainwater off his forehead. "Look. It's going to be easy," he said. He pointed.

Squinting into the darkness, I saw the canvas tarp over one side of the house. Their house-painting job was still underway.

"Why is it going to be easy?" I asked.

Then I saw the ladder, and I answered my own question.

A tall ladder leaned against the side of the house, tilting from the driveway up over the slanting roof.

"It's a piece of cake!" Shark declared, suddenly excited. "They left a ladder for us. A piece of cake! Let's go do this thing!"

Nikki held back. "Are you just going to climb into her bedroom? Won't she wake up?"

Shark pointed again. "That's her room up there. The one in the front. We'll climb into a room in the back. Then we can sneak into Candy's room quietly."

My breath caught in my throat. I suddenly had doubts. Lots of them.

I suddenly didn't want to be here.

"Shark, we didn't bring a flashlight or anything," I whispered, my eyes on the dark house. "How will we find her room?"

"I've been up there before. We can figure it out," he said.

"But . . . how will we find the amulet in the dark?" Nikki asked.

"No problem," Shark told her. "She wears it every day. So she probably leaves it out somewhere. We'll find it."

He snickered. "She'll wake up tomorrow morning, and it'll be gone. And when she comes to school, she'll see the big grins on our faces. And she'll know what a loser she is."

Was Shark really that sure of himself? Was he really that confident?

Or was he saying all that to cover up the fact that he was terrified too?

No time to think about it.

My jacket was soaked through. The cold rain pattered down harder.

Shielding my eyes with one hand, I followed Shark and Nikki up the driveway.

Shark and I each grabbed a side of the ladder. Luckily, it was aluminum and light enough for us to carry. We made our way to the back of the house.

No lights on back here, either. I spotted a partly open window on the second floor.

We carefully lowered the ladder to the back wall near that window.

Shark brushed raindrops from his hair. His expression was grim. His eyes were on the half open window. "Here goes," he said softly.

He grabbed the sides of the ladder and started to climb.

25

I followed Shark up the ladder. My legs felt rubbery and weak. I'd never broken into a house before.

I took a deep breath and held it, trying to slow my racing heart. Candy is all alone in there, I told myself. Her parents are away. We have her outnumbered three to one.

But she has the amulet.

My hands slipped on the wet metal ladder. I grabbed on tight and kept climbing. I glanced down and saw Nikki right behind me.

Above me, I saw Shark struggling with the window. He shoved it open and disappeared inside the house.

A few seconds later, I swung a leg over the windowsill and stepped inside. I turned and helped Nikki climb off the ladder.

The three of us stood very still. We were all breathing hard. My clothes were soaked through from the rain.

"Where are we?" Nikki whispered.

I glanced around, waiting for my eyes to adjust to the darkness. The room was hot and smelled kinda musty. After a few seconds, a bed came into focus, and a low dresser beside it. Cartons were stacked against one wall. I took a few steps forward and stumbled over an exercise bike piled high with folded clothes.

"Must be a spare bedroom or something," I whispered.

Shark made his way quickly to the door and pulled it open. Dim, yellow light flooded into the room. We tiptoed into a narrow hall. A ceiling light had been left on at the far end. It sent a dull, yellow glow over the dark-wallpapered hall.

We kept our backs pressed against the wall and moved silently, keeping close together. We passed a tiny room, probably a bathroom, and then closed double doors. A linen closet?

My chest ached. I could barely breathe. My eyes darted from side to side, alert to any movement.

We passed a framed photograph of a small cabin overlooking a lake. A small, square table with a tall flower vase on it. Another closet. We were walking away from the light. The hall grew darker.

We reached the stairway. Across from it—an open door.

"This is Candy's room," Shark whispered.

He didn't wait for us to react. He turned and disappeared into the room, moving silently. Nikki hung back. Even in the faint light, I could see the fear on her face.

"Wait out here," I whispered. "In case there's trouble."

It didn't make any sense. What could Nikki do if there was trouble? But I could see she was grateful for an excuse to stay in the hall.

I stepped into the doorway. The room smelled sweet, kinda flowery. It was pitch black. Just a little gray light slipping through the window curtains.

I swallowed hard. I had a huge lump in my throat that I couldn't swallow away. I took another step, then stopped when I saw Candy's bed.

I heard soft, steady breathing. It took me a

long moment to see Shark. I tiptoed over to him. The floorboards squeaked under me.

I stopped and turned to the bed. I heard Candy let out a sigh. Shark and I both froze.

Candy shifted in the bed. I could see the quilt move.

She didn't get up. The soft, steady breathing returned.

Shark hunched over a dressing table across from the bed. He picked up some items—cosmetics jars, I think—and silently moved things around.

A tall dresser stood beside the dressing table. The top drawer was half open. I turned to the dresser and peered inside. Sweaters and tops.

Shark pushed up beside me. "I've got it," he whispered in my ear. He held up a fist. "Let's go, Nate."

I stared at the closed fist. I froze for a moment. Shark had to give me a shove to get me going.

I stumbled into the hall. My shoes thudded on the wood floor. Shark came close behind. Nikki's eyes went wide with surprise.

Shark opened his fist and showed us the amulet.

Nikki gasped.

My heart pounded so hard, I couldn't say a word. All three of us stared at the amulet, the jewels glimmering in the dull light.

"Mission accomplished," Shark whispered. A wide grin spread over his face. He pointed to the stairway. "Let's go out the front door."

We were nearly to the stairs when a bright light flashed on.

I blinked and cried out.

Spinning around, I saw Candy in the doorway to her room. Her long nightshirt was twisted around her body. Her dark hair was tangled and matted wetly to her forehead.

"What are you DOING here?" she screamed. Her hands balled into tight fists. "Are you *crazy?* What are you doing here?"

Then her eyes stopped on the amulet in Shark's fist. Her mouth opened in a furious scream. "Give me that! Thief! Give it back!"

Nikki and I stumbled back from the stairway as Candy took a running leap. She grabbed the amulet from Shark's hand—

—and fell. Fell headfirst . . .

. . . headfirst down the stairs . . . screaming . . .

. . . screaming until her head smashed onto a wooden stair. I heard a horrifying *crack*.

Her body thudded hard against the wall. She tumbled down more steps. Did a wild somersault. I heard another loud *crack* as her head hit again.

I pushed past Shark and Nikki and stared down the stairwell, trembling in horror.

Get up, I silently prayed. Candy—get up!

But she didn't move.

Her body was twisted in an unnatural angle. One leg bent beneath her. Her head tilted to one side. Tilted *too far.* Her mouth open, eyes open wide.

"Get up! Get up!" I didn't realize I was screaming. "Candy—get up!"

And then all three of us flew down the stairs. And bent over her. And stared at her blank, lifeless eyes. And the bone—her neck bone—poking out from her skin.

She wasn't breathing.

She won't get up.

"I . . . I killed her," Shark stammered, backing against the side of the stairs.

"No—," Nikki protested. "It was an accident."

"You didn't do it, Shark," I said in a trembling voice. "Really. You didn't. It was an accident. Nikki and I saw the whole thing. It . . . it was an accident."

"It's so *horrible*!" Nikki cried, pressing her hands to her face. "But at least . . . at least she won't be able to do any more terrifying things to us. At least she won't be trying to kill us anymore."

Yes! The amulet.

I gasped as I saw it beneath Candy's open hand on the floor.

I reached down . . . reached over her dead body . . . and grabbed it.

"Come on!" I shouted. "We're safe now. We've got it. Let's get out of here!"

I took a deep breath. Then I took off, running out the front door with Nikki and Shark close behind me. My heart pounded as I tore down the driveway clutching the amulet.

We're safe, I told myself.

No more evil spells. No more evil magic.

Safe. Safe.

Then I stopped. Stopped at the curb. Gasping for breath.

Shark bumped into me. Nikki let out a startled cry.

"Nate—what's wrong?" Shark asked. "Hey, what is it?"

I held up the amulet. My hand trembled. "It . . . it . . ." I was panting too hard to talk.

Shark grabbed my arm. They both stared at the pendant in my hand.

At the *two pieces* of pendant in my hand.

"It . . . cracked in half," I finally choked out.

I held it up to them.

"It cracked in half because it's plastic. Don't you see? It's just plastic. It's a fake. Candy never had the real amulet. It's just a cheap, plastic fake."

26

"We did a horrible thing," I said. "We sneaked away. We closed the back window and pulled the ladder back to the side of the house. We didn't call the police or anything. We just sneaked away."

"You had no choice," Jamie said. "You could never explain what you were doing in Candy's house. No one would ever believe you."

It was a few nights later, and a group of us sat in the back booth at Nights. Jamie and Lewis held hands under the table. Shark was already on his third beer.

I felt totally tense. I mean, Candy was dead. But I didn't know whether we were safer now or not.

"We didn't kill her," Shark said in a whisper. "It really was an accident."

"You did the right thing," Lewis said. "If you stayed and called the police, your lives would be ruined forever. You'd be toast."

"Your lives would be over before they began," Jamie whispered.

Shark and I exchanged glances. We knew the memory of that night would haunt us forever.

The four of us talked some more. We tried to talk about other things. But how *could* we talk about anything else?

"Maybe we're all safe now," Lewis said. I saw him squeeze Jamie's hand. "Maybe the weird stuff is over."

"I hope you're right," I said. "Definitely hope you're right."

As I drove home through the dark, silent streets, I kept picturing Candy sprawled out so awkwardly, her head hanging limply on her broken neck. And I pictured the amulet . . .

. . . The fake, plastic amulet cracked in two pieces.

I crept into the house and moved silently up the stairs. Pale yellow light washed into my bedroom from the street light at the curb. I tugged off my jacket and tossed it to the floor.

I pulled my T-shirt over my head and tossed it down too. I turned to my bed.

And stopped.

In the pale light, I saw a lump under the covers. A big, round lump.

My balled-up pajamas? That was my first thought.

I strode over to the bed and pulled back the covers.

I gasped when I saw the round, dark puddle that stained the sheet.

Then I saw the pinkish ball. At first I thought it was a balloon. Or a sagging rubber ball.

Then I saw a floppy, pointed ear. Two round, black eyes staring up at me.

A hairy snout. Veins and tendons twisting like tentacles from a jagged, open throat.

And I realized I was staring at a head.

A fat, blood-smeared *hog's* head.

I staggered back, choking . . . choking . . . until finally, I found my voice. And then I opened my mouth wide in a high wail of horror.

TO BE CONTINUED

in FEAR STREET NIGHTS #2:
MIDNIGHT GAMES

R.L. Stine invented the teen horror genre with Fear Street, the bestselling teen horror series of all time. He also changed the face of children's publishing with the mega-successful Goosebumps series, which *Guinness World Records* cites as the Best-Selling Children's Books ever, and went on to become a worldwide multimedia phenomenon. The first two books in his new series Mostly Ghostly, *Who Let the Ghosts Out?* and *Have You Met My Ghoulfriend?* are *New York Times* bestsellers. He's thrilled to be writing for teens again in the brand-new Fear Street Nights books.

R.L. Stine has received numerous awards of recognition, including several Nickelodeon Kids' Choice Awards and Disney Adventures Kids' Choice Awards, and he has been selected by kids as one of their favorite authors in the National Education Association Read Across America. He lives in New York City with his wife, Jane, and their dog, Nadine.

Here's a sneak peek at
FEAR STREET NIGHTS #2:
MIDNIGHT GAMES

Just when Nate, Jamie, Lewis, and Shark
thought the Fear Street curse had lifted,
Dana Fear arrives in town. . . .

Screaming all the way, Ada thudded down the stairs.

The music and voices were so loud, but I could hear every *bump*, every time her head hit a wooden step.

And then the voices and singing and laughter stopped. As if someone had turned a switch. A few seconds after that, the music stopped too.

And now I felt as if I were swimming in silence, an ocean of silence. A bright white ocean of silence and light.

I grabbed the banister. I peered down through the billowing whiteness, forcing my eyes to focus.

And saw Ada. Crumpled up. Sprawled in a heap, surrounded by glittering lights. It took me a while to realize the lights were pieces of broken glass.

"Is she okay?" I screamed into the silence.

Kids were rushing to the stairway now, dropping down beside Ada. Brushing away the shards of shattered glass. Reaching for her. Eyes wide with worry and amazement.

Ada groaned. She slowly pushed herself up to a sitting position.

I saw bright red blood streaming down the front of her T-shirt and staining one sleeve. Bits of broken glass shimmered in her hair.

She groaned again and wiped her hands through her hair. Then, slowly, she raised her eyes to me.

I gasped when I saw the fierce anger on her face.

"You PUSHED me!" Ada screamed.

I heard gasps and low cries. All eyes were raised to me.

My legs felt wobbly, about to give way. I gripped the banister tightly to hold myself up. I felt my heart start to pound.

"N-no," I stammered, shaking my head. "I didn't touch you!"

Ada raised herself to her knees. She shook

a blood-smeared fist at me. "You DID, Dana!" she cried. "You shoved me!"

I couldn't help it. I burst into tears. "That's a LIE!" I cried. But my sobs muffled the words.

I gazed down from face to face. They all stared at me, accusing me. They *believed* her.

But I knew it wasn't true. I never touched her.

Why was she accusing me?

I couldn't stop sobbing. I turned and ran up the stairs. Back to my attic room, where I dropped into an armchair. I gripped the arms hard, gritted my teeth, and forced myself to stop crying.

From my room I could hear voices downstairs. But I couldn't make out the words. Were they all talking about me? Did they all believe Ada?

Why would I push her down the stairs? I had no reason to hurt her.

Did they think I pushed her because I want to steal Nate?

Nate is cute, but he isn't worth trying to *kill* someone!

Did they think I pushed her because I'm a Fear? And a member of the Fear Family *has* to be evil? How stupid is *that*?

I heard the front door close. Heard voices in the driveway. Car doors slammed, and engines started up. The party was breaking up.

I was still hunched in the armchair, gritting my teeth, thinking angry thoughts, when Jamie came into my room. She hurried over and placed a hand on mine. "Dana, are you okay?"

"I . . . don't know," I said. I felt like crying again, but I forced it back.

Jamie squeezed my hand. "It was a good party," she said softly, "until Ada fell."

"I didn't push her!" I cried. I jerked Jamie's hand off mine. "Really. I never touched her."

Jamie nodded. "Of course you didn't."

I jumped to my feet. I balled my hands into tight fists. "So why did she accuse me like that?"

Jamie tossed back her dark hair. She suddenly looked so pale and tired. I could see that blue vein throbbing in her temple. "Ada will get over it," she said.

"Get over it?" I cried. "How? If she thinks I tried to kill her . . ."

"She was being emotional," Jamie replied. "Ada is very high-strung. When she thinks about it, she'll realize she made a mistake. She tripped, that's all."

"I . . . I felt weird up there," I confessed. "I was standing behind Ada at the top of the stairs. And the glasses on her tray suddenly started to shine in my eyes. I felt dizzy."

"Dizzy?"

"Yes. I thought I might black out. But . . . you've got to believe me. I didn't push her. I couldn't."

"Of course not," Jamie said in a soft, soothing voice. "Of course not."

So why was she staring at me so suspiciously?

feel the fear.

FEAR STREET® NIGHTS

A brand-new Fear Street trilogy by the master of horror

R.L. STINE

In Stores Now

Simon Pulse
Published by Simon & Schuster
FEAR STREET is a registered trademark of Parachute Press, Inc.

FEAR STREET® —

WHERE YOUR WORST NIGHTMARES LIVE

R.L. STINE — FEAR STREET — ALL-NIGHT PARTY

R.L. STINE — FEAR STREET — THE CONFESSION

R.L. STINE — FEAR STREET — THE PERFECT DATE

R.L. STINE — FEAR STREET — KILLER'S KISS

R.L. STINE — FEAR STREET — THE RICH GIRL

R.L. STINE — FEAR STREET — THE STEPSISTER

By bestselling author

R.L. STINE

Simon Pulse
Published by Simon & Schuster
FEAR STREET is a registered trademark of Parachute Press, Inc.